ALIGNING ☆ STARS

MARCUS
IN RETROGRADE

S. A. SOMMERS

Marcus in Retrograde
All rights reserved.
Copyright 2019 © S.A. Sommers

Cover: JRA Stevens for Down Write Nuts
Formatting: Down Write Nuts

Excerpt from "UNTIED" by Katherine Rhodes used with permission from the author.

CHAPTER ONE

CHASE

THAT. FUCKING. DOG.

Bark! *Bark*! *Bark*! All night long.

I liked dogs just fine, but that miserable fleabag just kept barking, all night. I mean, we were on the sixth floor of the building, what the hell was there to bark about? A curtain? A chicken bone? Someone stole his pig's ear?

I'd buy him the whole hog if he'd just *shut up* for one night.

Staring up at the ceiling, I blew out a breath. I had thought that once Grumpy Grampa Able Woolworth had moved out from next door, I'd get some peace in my life.

Nope.

Now I had Growler the Barking Moron next door.

Just like with Able Woolworth, I knew that the landlord wasn't going to do shit about the dog. He never did shit about anything until we threatened to talk to the building owner or the city about the violations.

Mr. Hernandez, the owner, was awesome, though. We all got together and asked him for new windows last year, and had them in a month. He thanked us because the heating costs went down over the winter.

Right about now, though, I was ready to petition for sound proofing. I had two hours left before I had to get up to go to work, and I was listening to Lassie yipping about Timmy down the well.

This was stupid.

I sat up in the bed and ran a hand down my face. There was no point in this. I was going to have to try and sleep in the living room again for a few nights. If I had to switch the living room and bedroom I was going to be pissed—but not as pissed as I'd be if I couldn't get my sleep.

Grabbing the blanket and pillow I moved to the couch. Thank God I had made sure the thing was comfortable enough for sleeping when I bought it. I didn't think it would be me sleeping on it.

The two hours I had left flew by once I'd finally been far enough away from the damn dog to ignore him.

"Hey, Marcus, you look like shit!"

Patsy. I reached my hand out and shot her a middle finger, which immediately got her laughing. I took a sip of the tea in my hand and stumbled to my desk. I dropped into the chair and let out a sigh as I woke up the computer from sleep.

"Trouble sleeping, Chase?"

I tossed a look over my shoulder to my cubemate. Felix sat there, dressed to the nines in all the newest and hottest fashions, sporting nude lip gloss and just a little touch of eyeliner.

"What ever gave you that idea?"

"Because you look like you could carry my groceries home in those bags."

I fucking hated Felix Germaine. The man was a smarmy asshole who drank thirty dollar bottles of wine and ate at Wayan. I'd bet his lip gloss was from Bergdorf and his socks were silk.

"Piss off, Felix," I stated. "Where's your bear?"

He sniffed, and turned back around. "Aaron had to go to his parents this weekend, for family reasons. He'll be back tomorrow."

"Good, maybe he'll screw some of that arrogance out of you," I snapped.

He gave a distressed little yelp, and looked terribly offended that I would mention [whispering]: *sex* at his workplace. Whatever.

God, I could've used a good lay myself.

Sighing, I took another sip of my tea. I had a pile of work I needed to focus on, and it sucked being a half-awake graphic designer. Things didn't go as planned when the mouse slid across the screen as I jerked awake again.

"Coming out to get drinks tonight?"

I screamed and jerked so hard in my chair I slammed my knee on the desk. That sent a new string of swear words out of my mouth as I grabbed my now-throbbing joint.

"For the love of God and Baby Jesus, Jeri," I growled.

"You woke him up." Felix chuckled.

"Did I?" Jeri asked. "Dude, you shouldn't come out with us tonight." She paused a beat. "Are you coming out?"

"Honey, he already came out," Felix said, "he just forgot to get dressed while he was in the closet."

"Felix!" I snapped. "Yes, Jeri, I am coming out tonight. Maybe the stupid dog will have shut up by the time I get home."

"Dog?"

"My neighbor has a dog and it just keeps barking."

"Landlord?"

"Oh please," I groaned. "Don't you remember the toilet incident?"

"Ooh, that's right." Jeri grimaced. "He's a useless jackass. Got it. What are you gonna do? You can't keep falling asleep at the desk."

"If it happens again, I guess I'll give him a warning."

"Mmm."

I lifted an eyebrow. "Mmm? What does that mean?"

"You're going to need help to switch the living room and bedroom."

"No I'm not."

I totally was.

I almost gave in and asked her for her husband's help moving things, but then I thought of one more option.

Shame. Maybe I could shame the guy into keep his dog quiet. There were ways to do that and I was sure other people in the building would be right there with me about that *bark bark barking.*

But it would have to be fun. Or funny. I was always a little bit chicken when it came to confronting people about things that inconvenienced me. My mother had said I was more Canadian than American when it came to my 'ope, sorry!' policy.

And...I ruined my morning thinking about my mother.

Yay.

"SO AFTER he whips the container of floss out and pulls out like two feet of it," Noah said, "he starts flossing at the table like his life depended on it."

"At Per Se?" Jeri asked.

Noah nodded. "At the table at Per Se."

We were all trying not to laugh. Noah had the worst luck dating. His brother Uriah made a *go on* motion because he—and the rest of us—didn't trust ourselves not to burst out laughing.

"Well, his dentist must be proud because he cleaned his teeth so well, I swear they were squeaking." The poor guy let out a sigh. "The dessert comes out and he's staring at it like it had a Face Hugger in it. It was a fabulous looking chocolate dome, the kind they melt with a warm sauce to reveal the real dessert inside. He sits back and shakes his head. 'No, no, no. I said I wanted fruit.'"

"Fruit. At Per Se," I managed.

"I was so tempted to ask the waiter to get him a side of apples from McDonald's down the street." Noah shook his head. "I was so glad he was picking up the tab." He leaned his cheek on his fist. "I thought."

"Oh, my God, no," Lena gasped.

Slowly, Noah nodded. "Yep."

"Dine and Ditch?" Jeri asked.

"Oh, no. No. He *forgot his wallet.*"

That was the end of us. We collapsed into roaring laughter as poor, feckless Noah smirked and chuckled at his own misfortune. The poor guy had been on so many bad dates over the years I'd known him, most of us had told him to write a book about them.

"So what happened?" Jeri asked.

"I had *not* forgotten my card. I paid. Through the ass, I might add, which was why I didn't want to go on a first date to Per Se. But he went and made reservation and brought the floss."

I nudged him with my elbow. "How much?"

He canted his head and stared at me. "With or without the glass of Chateau d'Yquem?"

"Holy shit," Lena exclaimed. "He did not."

Once again, Noah nodded slowly. "He did."

"Total bill," Uriah said, prompting him.

I saw the pain in my friend's eyes. "Nine hundred fourteen dollars and thirty-three cents."

Everyone sitting around us whistled.

Uriah leaned forward. "It gets better."

"Worse, Uri...it gets *worse*." Noah let out a long-suffering sigh. "I pay half my rent to get out of this restaurant and get out of this date, right? And we get outside and he asks if I can call *and pay for* an Uber."

"No. Way," Jeri said, calming down enough to interject. "What did you do?"

"I pulled out my wallet, hand him a five and a condom and told him to go get fucked." He folded his arms.

We all burst out laughing again, and I held up my hand for a high-five. He obliged after a moment and joined in the laughter.

It was only the latest in the long line of poor Noah's terrible track record with dating. He just couldn't seem to find the kind of guy he could even get home to bed with, never mind a second date. And if he did get to a second date, it was the disaster the first one had managed to avoid.

"How was Felix after I stopped by?" Jeri asked a few minutes later.

"Just as rude and awful as you can imagine. That guy needs to be slapped off his pedestal, and soon," I answered. "Most of the time, the other gay guys I meet are supportive and there's no competition. He's just terrible. He's a total mean girl."

"Just remember that on Wednesday, he wears pink." Jeri giggled.

"Yeah, a pink thong." I sighed.

Jeri looked terrified. "You're kidding."

"Oh, no, I'm not. I've seen him when he comes back from a lunch time shopping trip to wherever he gets that shit from uptown."

"Oh, that was more than I needed to know..." She grabbed her beer and took a swig from the glass. "So, do you need me and Dan to come over and help you switch the rooms this weekend?"

I stared at her, and then slumped in the chair. "Damn it. No. I'm not giving up this fight yet. I'm going to see if I can publicly shame him into teaching the dog to hush."

"You sure?"

"Yes." I nodded once. "But keep next weekend open."

CHAPTER TWO

MARCUS

POLLUX PULLED THE LEASH SO HARD I was sure he had pulled my shoulder out of it's socket. Where this little thirty pound mutt got his power, I had no idea, but at the end of the leash, he was dangerous.

I finally managed to answer the phone ringing in my hand after getting him back under control.

"Hello?"

"Hi, Marcus!" My mother's happy tones came through, and it brightened my mood immediately.

"Hey, Mom," I answered, carefully checking both directions on the one way street. I had learned that the hard way when I was almost taken out by a taxi at two in the morning.

"How's the new place?"

"I have a couch, TV and bed, Mom. Same as when I left. I'm living out of cardboard boxes and Hungry

Man microwave meals are as gourmet as I'm getting right now."

"You really need a dresser, Marcus. Why don't Dad and I drive down this weekend."

"Mom. Stop. It's fine. I knew this was the way it was going to be when I moved down here. I'm okay with it. The point was not a dresser, the point was the job."

"Right, right." she admitted. "How's that going?"

I chuckled. "Same as it was yesterday, Mom."

She laughed. "Okay, all right. I might miss having you around the house a bit, Marcus. I'm suffering empty nest."

"Charlene and the kids are three blocks away. I'm sure she'd be happy to send her beasts over to you once in a while to remind you why young people have kids and older people retire and have empty nests."

She started laughing. "I know, I know. I just miss coffee and bagels with my boy."

"Aw." I swooned a bit. I was totally my mom's favorite and I knew it. I didn't try to exploit it though. "You knew this had to happen. I couldn't make it as a voice actor in Troy."

"You were doing fine with the books," she said, sadly, but I knew she was playing the guilt card at this point.

"Yes, but I can't just live on books, Mom. If I ever want to do movies, I have to be closer to the action." I smiled and pulled Pollux back on his leash, away from the over-groomed Pomeranian he was currently sniffing in consideration for a hump. "I'm still doing the books anyway, and they haven't let me near their editing equipment yet. I'm still in training."

"Training? Four years of college..."

"It's orientation, Mom. Just showing me around, getting me used to the place, the people, the policies. Next week, I'll start shadowing their Vivid editor."

"And how's my granddog doing?" I could hear the laughter in her voice.

"He's peeing on every tree and making New York his," I answered.

God, I loved my parents. They were just the best and I was so lucky to have them. Even though I knew Mom was honest about her missing me, I also knew that she and Dad were proud of me, and they were willing to do anything for my two older sisters.

Charlene, Christy-Anne, and I had sat down when I made the decision to move to New York City. It was time for our parents to enjoy retirement, and they were young enough to do that. We all knew Mom lived for her kids—she was an award winning math teacher after all. So not having any of us at home was going to be tough. Charlene promised to bring the grandkids over often. Christy-Anne promised she would take Mom out to coffee at least once a week, and I promised I would always answer the phone and do my best to visit once every two months.

I'd been in the city a week. Mom called every day. Dad called every night. It was just so *them*.

"And how about you, Marcus? Found anyone worth marking?"

"Mom, ew. I don't pee on my dates."

"Marcus Chastain Romano, ew."

We both burst out laughing. She might have been an award winning teacher, but that was math. English was fun with her. She tried to be funny, but often accidently made a sexual innuendo. Which was fun once the three of us were old enough to get the jokes that had often sent my father running for a napkin to prevent a spit-take.

"All right, Mom, I gotta get going. Pollux looks like he's ready to wine and dine every bitch on the block and I don't think the owners would appreciate that. I'll talk to Dad tonight."

"You're avoiding my question, Marcus!"

"Gotta go, bye!" I called, teasing her and closing the connection.

She'd laugh the rest of the day. I would too. Mom really thought I was a smooth operator and would have lured the partner of my choice to my bed and my life in the first two days I was here.

I hadn't even been to the bar down the street yet. Moving, new job, creating the audiobooks—I was exhausted.

Pollux, thankfully, had decided he was done pissing on every tree and hydrant. He did his business near the curb and I quickly picked it up with the bio-degradable bag, and chucked it in the trash bin on the corner.

I headed up the stairs with my dog, and stopped dead on the landing for my floor. There, on the common billboard, was my apartment number written in red at the top of a piece of paper.

One week. Just one week and they already didn't like me?

I walked up to the paper and my eyebrows hit the top of my hairline at the message. It was actually... really well drawn.

Dear Neighbor in 302—

I appreciate you being an animal lover, but most people agree that a barking dog at three a.m. negates most of that love and appreciation. Sorry, but you got to keep him quiet.

Your neighbor,

301

And there under the short note was a picture of what was clearly a German Shepherd, looking sad and sporting a very dog-friendly basket muzzle.

Which also meant that the artist, no doubt my neighbor 301, didn't really want me to muzzle Pollux, but to generally shut him up.

I took the sheet off the bulletin board and shoved it in my back pocket and stepped to my door. Unlocking and stepping inside, I eyed the dog.

"Dude. Are you barking in the middle of the night?" I asked him. As if he could answer me. He dropped his haunches to the ground and stared at me.

How could he be barking in the middle of the night and I couldn't hear it? That was bad on several different, important levels. Pollux was a good guard dog. Very good. He had an instinct for not barking at just anything and everything, so when he did, there was usually an actual threat. And next, I wasn't waking up to his accurate barking. That scared me because if I didn't wake up to his bark, what said that I would ever hear the smoke alarm, or someone busting in the front door?

I was a rural kid, and I had to talk myself out of thinking that everyone was going to break into my apartments. Pollux helped that.

Taking his leash off, I refilled his water bowl and sat down at the small folding table that served as a kitchen table. I pulled the note out of my pocket and studied it.

The art was actually really cute. The dog looked like he was sad and sorry at the same time, and it was clear that the artist in 301 didn't want to go to the landlord about me.

Of course, 301 could have just knocked on the door and talked to me. That would've been the polite and neighborly thing to do, instead of calling me out like that. I wondered if anyone else had seen it.

I also wondered if 301 was home and we could chat about this in person. Glancing at Pollux, slopping water all over the floor as usual, I nodded. "Let's see if we can solve this like a gentleman."

Just as my hand wrapped around the doorknob, I froze. What if the artist in 301 was like the last boyfriend I had? What if he was like Ed? What if he took my innocent request to talk as some kind of invitation? If anything happened to him, or I was in the house with him alone for too long, it would be

Boston Conservatory all over again.

So I chickened out. Again.

It seemed ridiculous for the star linebacker of his high school football team to be just such a fucking chicken about facing a neighbor. But all I could think of was how I'd barely made it out Boston with my degree.

Forget my dignity, that had been shredded.

I chewed on my lip. Now what the hell did I do? I had to deal with the barking and the complaint, but I was stuck behind the wall of my own damn fears.

I glanced at Pollux who was now dutifully licking his butt. I rolled my eyes, and sat back down at the table. Tapping my finger on the note, I studied it.

A moment later, I grabbed a pen and some paper. I wasn't such a bad artist myself.

☆

"ARE YOU liking the city?" Sorcha asked, spinning a knob on the sound equipment.

"So far so good," I answered. "Just getting my bearings and getting everything sorted. I think I have the commute down pat, and I'm trying to find a decent grocery. I'm used to Price Chopper."

She stopped and looked up at me. "Excuse me what?"

Chuckling, I nodded. "Price Chopper. Great name, isn't it. I don't know what dingbat branded that, but we're all used to it up there."

"Well, there you go." She turned back to the soundboard. "I would recommend D'Agostinos, but honestly, if you can find the fruit and veggie bodega and a bakery, you really only need them for things like meat and cheese."

"A man does not need more than meat and cheese!"

Sorcha busted out laughing. "Okay, Captain Caveman, chill with the testosterone."

I chuckled. "Actually, I love fruit and vegetables. So thank you for reminding me about the markets. I'm not a vegetarian, but I don't go to Delmonico's and eat a thirty-two ounce steak as a habit."

"Look at you, learning the city's fancy restaurants off the bat." She grinned.

"Gotta know where I can't afford to eat right now."

She nodded, then studied me. "Are you paying attention to what I'm doing at all?"

"Well..." I drew out the word and coughed at the end.

"You already know how to do all this, don't you?"

"I do..."

She was suspicious, and I had the feeling I was about to be outed. "Why do I think it's not just something you picked up in school?"

"It wasn't. I have a working set up in my place."

Her jaw dropped. "For audio?"

"Yes."

It was quiet a moment, then she cocked her head. "Why?"

"I do independent audiobook narration."

This time, she rotated the whole chair around to look at me. "Holy. Shit. You're *that* Marcus?

Chastain?"

"Well, my real last name *is* Romano, but I ask to be published and distributed by Chastain. Simply because I didn't want to take the chance that someone would know my name and recognize my voice."

"Dude. I listen to your books all the time," Sorcha gasped. She flushed bright red, and I knew what was going to come out of her mouth. "You have the most amazing bedroom voice ever..."

I shook my head and pinched the bridge of my nose. "Yeah. I've been told. At least you were discreet about it."

"People aren't discreet?"

I laughed. Hard. "Are you kidding? I've had more women come up to me and ask me to talk to them just so they could—uh...Jill off in the bathroom."

"Jill off?!" She couldn't stop laughing. "Oh, my God, you're precious. None of them offered more?"

"They all offer more," I said. "But I'm gay, so it doesn't do shit for me."

She gasped and put a hand to her chest. "Oh, no! Did you hear that? It was the sound of millions of hearts breaking!" The grin never left her face and she dropped her hand back to the board. "Actually, I kind of figured you were."

"How?" I asked.

"Gaydar, my friend. Gaydar."

"That's pretty strong. I've always been told that I let off a pretty strong straight vibe."

Sorcha shook her head. "You've never met anyone as straight as me, my friend. I have like zero interest in the same sex. I have trouble finding even the most beautiful woman slightly more than objectively beautiful. I can suss out even the smallest amount of bicuriosity in anyone. And you are not bi. You are lighting up my gay-board like a Christmas tree." She made little flashy motions with her hands.

"Usually people who say they are that straight..."

"Don't you fret, Marcus. I'm an ally. I couldn't give a shit what you do with your boy bits in your down—or up—time. Just because my pendulum is stuck in the upside of the swing doesn't mean I don't get it." She patted my arm and flipped a few switches on the editing board. "Sex is awesome. Get you some."

I couldn't stop laughing. "I have the feeling that this job is going to work out just fine."

"And remember, I'm so straight that we can appreciate a fine male together."

"Bonus!"

"All right, Mister Women-Jill-Off-to-My-Voice," she said, pushing back from the editing board, "if you know what you're doing, why don't you show me." Sorcha held out the set of headphones she'd been using. "Back track and see if you can match me."

Sliding my chair over, I exaggeratedly cracked my knuckles—actually hurting one of my fingers—and wound back the track so I could listen to the whole thing. I knew she was working on putting natural water sounds for a scene in a show, and I had to hear what she had done to that point before I could pick it up.

She was good and this was what I had been dying to do for a while. I loved voice work, but I also loved working the soundboards. I listened a few more times, and finally caught her pattern, and started laying down more special effects.

"How long do we need the effects in this for?"

"The whole scene," she answered. "Another four minutes."

I lost myself in the board and watching for perfect places to drop different kinds of water sounds to make the whole thing seem natural. It took me twenty minutes to layer in the sound the way I wanted, and that blended with hers.

I put the headset down, and smiled. "There."

She pointed to the screen and speakers. "Show me."

I keyed it up to the marker and let it go. The switch from her tracks to mine was flawless, and while there were a few things I noticed outside the headset that I wanted to adjust, I was reasonably pleased with the track.

The clip ended and Sorcha was staring at the screen, tapping a finger on her chin. She was quiet and I couldn't read her at all. I was ready to hide under the soundboard before she finally spoke up.

"I'm getting Jerry to give you a room tomorrow. You don't need any tutoring on this, man. That was flawless and damn near perfect." She swiveled in the chair. "Ed is going to approve it on the first pass, and if you can get past Ed Roberts on the first pass, you're golden. There's a reason they always give me his stuff. He likes what I do. Well, now he has two of us."

My stomach dropped a little and I hoped that it didn't show on my face. "Ed Roberts?"

"Notoriously hard to work with," she said. "He's

an up and coming producer and he's a bit of prima donna and why do you now look like you're going to barf?"

I coughed, and covered my mouth. "I uh...my stomach went sour. Sorry about that. I need to grab some tums. Do you mind?"

"Go on. I'm going to go find Jerry and talk to him about you and your own editing room."

I nodded and tried to leave the room calmly. I hoped it work. I made it all the way to the bathroom, managed to lock the stall, and proceeded to heave up all of my lunch and swore half of my breakfast.

Not caring that this was a public bathroom, I leaned my forehead on the stall divider, absorbing the cool of the metal on my skin.

Ed Roberts.

I had just mixed a segment for Ed Roberts.

I heaved again, and this time, it was all bile, and I wasn't sure that I was done gagging yet.

All at once I had impressed my mentor enough that she felt like I didn't need more mentoring, and at the same time, I had a horrid realization that yes, Ed was in the same field as I was now and we were totally going to cross paths. Possibly often.

There had to be a way that I could avoid him. In all likelihood, Sorcha would be the one going to see him about the track, not me. But if I had my own studio and own assignments, at some point I was going to have to see him.

There was the rest of the gagging. Was this going to happen every time I had to deal with him?

Shit.

CHAPTER THREE

CHASE

THERE WAS A NOTE ON THE BULLETIN board where mine had been. I'd used red marker, and this one was in blue. It very clearly said *To 301*.

Oh, goodie. We were passing notes like we were in kindy-garten again.

Plucking it off the wall, I headed into the apartment. I chuckled as I dropped my messenger bag on the floor by the door. I hadn't brought any work home that night, because I'd managed to finish most everything I had on my desk on deadline.

Also, Felix had been out, so I didn't have to deal with his sniping. That was a relief. I hated that we shared that cube. There was nothing about that man that was likeable and I was over it.

Looking at the note in my hand, I made myself a promise to go talk to management about changing my desk location. There had to be another open desk on the floor where I didn't have to deal with Gayzilla all day.

Opening the paper, I found my neighbor's response to the damn barking dog.

Dear 301,

Pollux is a willful, free spirit and I cannot contain his joy and delight at simple things like bugs, curtains and air moving around his head. I would not want to contain it, because it is joy on an ethereal level. Sorry if he barks.

Your Neighbor 302 and Pollux

The dog was named Pollux.

And my neighbor was an arrogant jerk.

Under the note was a more than serviceable drawing of a much smaller dog than the German shepherd I'd imagined, leaping off the ground with his idiot tongue hanging out, and look of pure, stupid, doggy bliss on his face. His leash swung free, he wore a crown of flowers, and there was a fire hydrant on the other side from the leash.

Well, Neighbor 302 could draw, I'd give them that. And I'd give them another night with Pollux the Wunderhund. It was all my sanity could afford between the dog and Felix.

Glancing at the clock, I gasped. I didn't have a lot of time to get ready. Grabbing my phone out of my pocket I checked the text messages.

I let out a breath of relief.

Kieran: *Hey, sexy. You ready for this?*

I smiled and wrote back. *Been ready.*

He and I had been chatting for nearly two months, at first just online, then through text and just two weeks ago, we actually moved up to the phone. We were clicking in a major way and tonight we got to try our in-person chemistry.

Kieran had been so patient with me. It was one of the worst things about me—that I had to form a personal connection or sex didn't happen. He'd been willing to do that, and there were not many men who would.

I could not wait. I needed to get laid and soon. My right wrist was sore and even my left hand was getting familiar at this point. I was feeling good about the two of us working well together, and just maybe I might get myself a boyfriend. Finally.

I rushed through my refresh and clean up, and rushed out the door. I was going to have to take the time to come up with a witty retort to the neighbor's message at some point, but right now, I just ran down the stairs and out to the subway to catch the train.

I'd lived in New York City for five years and I'd never been to Delmonico's. I had been dying to go the whole time. Kieran suggested it because if we didn't hit it off, at least we would have had a date at one of the oldest and best restaurants in the city. We'd even agreed to go half because it wasn't a cheap place and we both had rent to pay.

I laughed at the rent again. Poor Noah. We'd actually all wound up giving him about fifty dollars apiece to help him recover a bit. He wasn't hard up for cash, but that had been an unfair situation and none of us wanted him to have to tap his savings for his rent.

We all paid through the ass to stay in Manhattan. It still wasn't as bad as Brooklyn, and while some of my friends were doing okay over in Jersey, we were all paying exorbitant rents. It was easy to see why people moved way out.

I'd lucked into my place, just below Bleaker near Washington Square, so the ride to the restaurant wasn't going to be very far or long. A quick walk to the Bleaker stop and down five to Wall Street, then two blocks more on foot. Easy peasy.

Standing just outside the restaurant was Kieran, looking like a perfect gentleman. He looked exactly like his pictures and I was glad. It meant I'd lucked into a fairly honest—and hot—guy.

"Chase?" He perked up as I approached, and a smirk graced his lips.

"Kieran," I said, sticking my hand out for him to shake.

He did. It was a firm, kind grip with a lot of confidence. I liked it. It was comforting.

"It's so good to finally meet you." He smiled and motioned to the door of the restaurant. "I'm looking forward to dinner. Shall we?"

I nodded and he held the door for me.

"Come up for a coffee?" I managed to force the words from my lips.

I hadn't been sure I was going to ask him up at all until that moment. Dinner had been amazing, and I'd really started to feel a connection with the guy. We weren't off the charts hot, but there was chemistry there. I couldn't keep putting off chances to find a good guy while waiting for the perfect man. Because on top of waiting for him, he'd also have to wait on me.

Kieran was hot. Smart, polite, kind. All of it. He was also patient and interested. If we took this to the bed, I was sure he wasn't going to be a fuck and flee.

Smiling, he nodded. "I'd love to."

We walked up to the building, and he stopped. "Wait. This is your place?"

I looked at the door and then back to him. "Yes?"

"You seriously live across the street from 177 Bleeker Street?"

"Oh...no..."

Kieran started laughing. "Please, please tell me a wizard doctor in a red cape lives there?"

I put a hand to my forehead. "The second floor is an adorable newlywed couple. The third is two NYU students, and the fourth is a single businessman."

"You memorized it?"

"Everyone who makes the connection wants to know if Stephen Strange lives there. I mean, does it *look* like a wizard lives there? Would you live there if you were a wizard? There are much nicer brownstones and Gilded Age mansions uptown."

Kieran tossed his head back and let out a resounding laugh. I pushed the door to my building open and led him inside. I chuckled along with him as we walked in.

We headed up the stairs to my apartment door. I glanced at the bulletin board and didn't see another note. The light was on under the door and I sighed softly.

I really hoped the dog didn't put the kaibosh on whatever was about to happen.

I had ideas.

Walking in, I flipped on the lights for the kitchen and headed in, pulling out a chair. "You like regular coffee or something different. I have hazelnut and macadamia, light roast and a Kona someone was nice enough to bring back from Hawaii."

"Plain old coffee is fine with me," he answered, sitting down on the chair I had offered. "You really know who lives across the street?"

"Yeah, there's a bell directory. I looked."

He chuckled and loosened his tie a bit, releasing the first button. I thought I should take a moment to appreciate what he as showing me, but my eyes slid to their task.

Damn it, libido! The good-looking guy we've been getting to know is here. Could you wake the fuck up?

Kieran cleared his throat. "So, now that we're not in public anymore, can I ask you a few more personal questions? I didn't want other people eavesdropping at the restaurant. Most people are fine, but I didn't want to chance it."

I nodded. "I get it." As accepted as the LGBTQ+ community was in the city—hell, I even lived in

Greenwich Village—you just never knew when one of the big mouths was listening. Also, no one needed to know our business.

Once again, it seemed like I should have a snide internal dialogue that sniped with things like, *Mmm but I sure would like to get into Kieran's business.*

But, alas, the sleeping, lazy fuck of a libido did not stir. Also, I sucked at internal Shakespearean soliloquy. But ask me to draw Aladdin and Jasmine and you'd have them in minutes.

"You're a gray-romantic..." he started. "I, being terribly curious, read everything on the internet about it because you're a hot piece of man and I would like to tap it. I understand that's not how it works with you."

"Not even close," I said, trying to keep the anger at myself out of my voice.

"How did you find out you were a gray-romantic?"

"By not reacting sexually to men in real life. I was only interested in my fictional gay romance heroes that I learned about through the course of a book."

"So, no porn?"

"Unless it has a story."

Kieran started laughing. "Stories in porn. That's a good one. They stopped trying that in the early 80s."

"And no one online has a clue that there are people who aren't into the *drill his ass by mark-thirty* guideline." God, I was making coffee and talking porn with a really hot guy who clearly wanted me and there was still nary a wiggle in the willy.

Christ, I was so broken.

"So, how do you handle...self...uh..."

I chuckled, and turned the coffee pot on. "Books. Lots and lots of books. I love series because I get to know the characters and then when they get lucky in the book, I have a conversation with Martin Palm and his five brothers."

That had him throwing his head back with a loud laugh. I could see his Adam's apple bobbing with his boisterous laugh, and...

Oh. Hello, libido. It's about time you woke up.

"So you have a really big collection of books then?"

"I'm an expert at left hand reads on my ereader." I opened the fridge and pulled out half and half, then brought it and the sugar to the table.

He was still laughing at the left hand joke as I found two mugs in the cabinet and put them on the counter. I took a deep breath and turned, leaning back. "Kieran, thank you for being patient with me. It's so hard to get guys to understand I can't just hop in the sack. No matter how much I want to, no matter how much I try to explain."

He lifted his lips into a small smile. "Are you kidding? Meeting a guy who wasn't there just for a hookup was a miracle. Most men assume that because I'm trans, I'm just a freak in the sheets and in the briefs and..." He sighed. "It's hard. It's all just really hard to get someone to realize I'm not a freak, and I'm not into fuck and flee. Not when I have so much baggage."

"I'm getting too old to play the games," I agreed. "Nothing comes easy."

"Well, *some* people come easy." He chuckled.

The coffee pot beeped at me that it was done brewing, and I quickly poured the two mugs. Setting the coffee pot to warm, took the hot drinks to the table. I put one down in front of Kieran, and took a deep breath. "Wanna watch a movie?"

He nodded and grabbed the half and half. "I'd like that."

We both dressed the coffee the way we liked and on the way to the living room, I kicked off my shoes and took off the tie.

I hoped that Kieran got the idea.

I also hoped my libido was paying attention.

"Let's see," Kieran said, picking up the remote. "If I remember correctly, you like sci-fi, superheroes, and Hallmark romance."

I coughed and blushed. "I like more than that..."

He elbowed me and had a cheesy grin on. I blushed harder.

"So, cable or streaming?"

"Oh streaming," I said. "I'm too busy and flighty to deal with cable."

Flicking on the TV, Kieran found the services I had and navigated to the screens he wanted. He was on a mission and in seconds he had *Jupiter Ascending* on the screen.

I laughed. "Okay, Channing Tatum. I can do that."

"I'd tag in on that," he said, and we both cracked up laughing in the next moment.

Just a few minutes into the movie, he lost all subtly, and just flat out put his arm around me and started playing with my hair. It felt so nice, and sent a little shiver of delight through me.

That was something I hadn't experienced in a while. Deciding to throw caution into a mild breeze, I snuggled into the crook of his arm. He was very comfortable, and my hand found his flat stomach and I traced my fingers over him through the shirt.

Mm, muscles.

His hand found my cheek and he turned me toward him. His lips were plump and looked like he had just wet them. They shown in the low light of the television screen.

Then, they were on mine.

At first, the kiss was sweet and soft. Almost chaste, but not quite when he opened his lips. I opened mine, and the warmth that passed between us was enough for the moment.

The moment passed quickly, and we turned into each other. His tongue sought out mine and he tasted like coffee and mocha. He was delicious and intoxicating, and my brain was into this.

It had been a very, very long time since I'd been interested enough in a man to kiss him. Kieran was a perfect gentleman, and he was so willing and able to take things at my pace. He kissed like a dream, sharing the power of it with me, let me lead and then insisting on leading me.

I pulled back, and kept my eyes closed as I dropped my head against the back of the couch. "Goddamn it," I hissed.

I heard a laugh and opened one eye to find Kieran with a hand over his mouth in a grin. Picking my head up, I raised an eyebrow.

His lips pursed as he dropped his hand. "Hmm."

"What hmm?" I asked.

"No spark."

Rotating on the cushion, I faced him. "What?"

"You kiss like a god, but...no spark."

I sat up. "No spark?"

Kieran looked sheepish. "No spark, Chase. I'm sorry. I didn't—"

Slapping my hand on his chest, I stopped him. "No. No, it's fine. There was no spark here either. You're handsome and you'd be an awesome boyfriend, but..."

His shoulders slumped. "Well, thank God we're on the same page here."

"But, Kieran, I don't want you to just walk away and never talk to me again because we aren't going to sleep together. I also happen to think you'd be an awesome friend to keep around."

He nodded. "I totally agree with that assessment."

"Good," I said, sitting back on the couch. "Coffee is coffee, and Channing Tatum is still Channing Tatum."

"Agreed. Maybe I'll have you over next and we can watch *Magic Mike*."

"I think that sounds like an awesome plan."

I settled back and let out a breath. Damn libido. Damn fouled sparkplugs. Damn it all. It was back to my gay erotic romance books and my left hand for a while.

The damn dog barked all night.

CHAPTER FOUR

MARCUS

THE GUY CAME SPRINTING OUT of the building, looking like hell. He had half a jacket on, and was trying to knot up his tie.

I yanked Pollux out of the way and laughed quietly.

He heard me, and stopped at the curb. Looking left and right, he finally let his shoulders slump and turned back to me. "It's a run of shame, okay? Subway?"

I pointed east down the street and he waved a thanks as he sprinted off.

"Well, Pollux, I guess it's all a balance. You get lucky the night before, you don't get so lucky in the morning."

He barked and peed on the hydrant in front of the building. He'd already peed his way through

Washington Square, so he was probably just remarking his territory. Heading up the stairs, I saw the red numbers on the bulletin board.

Wait, it was my turn for the note.

I looked down at Pollux. "Dude, you didn't bark all night again, did you?"

He whined and sat his ass in front of my door. Rolling my eyes, I grabbed the note. Pollux trotted in happily once I opened the door.

I took off his leash, hanging it up. I had enough time for a shower and breakfast and once more to the curb with the miserable barking disaster.

Unfolding the paper in my hand, I sighed. It was a picture of Pollux—no, it was a lot of pictures of Pollux, all of them barking and in several states of distress, insanity, concern, hunger, and pee-need.

Dear 302,

Could you please consider getting your pooch some doggy Xanax? How about doggy Benadryl? Or perhaps doggy Ambien? ...Well, no. Skip the Ambien. I don't want to know what dogs do on that stuff.

I need your puppers to be quiet. I do. He barks against my wall. I don't want to escalate this to management. I don't have the haircut for that. Could we try something, please?

Your Neighbor 301

Doggy Xanax. Seriously?

Still, the neighbor—a woman by the haircut comment?—was right. I couldn't let the mutt just yammer against the walls all night. Someone either above or below was going to get into the act with her and report me to the landlord. I didn't want to send Pollux back to my parents.

I ducked into the shower and hosed off as fast as I could. I felt like I swallowed my breakfast whole before I took Pollux back out for a quick pee break and then headed off to work.

Today I was taking a long lunch for a date. My first official date in New York City. The guy had been quietly eyeballing me at a meeting the day before and it only took him most of the day to ask me out.

He was really cute, and really unsure if I was gay, or into twinky guys. I didn't so much care about effeminate or not. I wanted a fun personality.

Ashton seemed like he might have that. It didn't hurt that he had a nice ass.

I leaned down and scratched Pollux behind the ears. "Listen, bud. Get your bark out during the day when no one is around. I don't want to piss off the neighbors any more than we have. We got a great deal on this place and we need it. I don't want to find a new place, and I don't want to commute more than I already do."

He yipped and walked away from me, hopping up on the couch and circling a few times to settle down. Idiot. Adorable, fuzzy idiot.

Sorcha met me at the door of her studio, leaning against the wall. She had a giant smile on her face, and barred me from going into her studio like I had been.

"You got your own board, Marcus. I showed the boss what you did the other day and he was tickled pink." She tossed a chin down the hall to her left. "You're in the studio beside me, and you'll find all your assignments in the mailbox on the front of the door every morning."

My jaw dropped. I'd been here just under two weeks.

"You're lying."

She pointed down the hall. "I'm not, go look."

I walked down to the next door. There, on the frosted class, was my name. *Marcus C. Romano, Sound Eng.*

I whipped my phone out and took a picture as Sorcha doubled over in laughter. While she was trying to compose herself, I texted the picture to half the damn planet.

"Go in, jackass." She held up a pair of keys.

Snatching them out of her hand, I unlocked the door and pushed it open.

I stepped into my own studio.

"This is amazing," I breathed.

"Feel free to fill it up with pictures of hot guys," she said from the door way.

"I'd never get anything done if I did," I answered. "Door would have to be locked at all times."

"Ew!" She laughed. Taking a few steps in, she clapped me on the shoulder. "Congrats, man. Seriously. You're good at what you do, and you don't need tutoring from the likes of me. Assignments are on the door, and you know how to access the filing system. Go to it, Marcus. Knock their socks off."

"Only if they use Gold Bond," I mumbled.

Her head bobbed in approval of my stupid joke. "You up for lunch?"

Sliding my eyes back over to her, I shook my head in the negative. "Not today."

"Why? Hot date?"

"Yes."

That made her laugh. "Ashton finally got up the nerve to ask you!"

"He did."

She headed for the door. "Good. He's been eyeballing your ass for the past four days." She looked back at me. "Not that I blame him." With a wink, she was gone.

I was really, really starting to like that woman.

Turning a small circle, I looked around. This was *my* studio. This was my workspace. Even some of the best sound engineers I knew didn't get their own space—they had to share and book studio time. I didn't, not anymore.

This was amazing. It seemed this move was going to be working out better than I thought.

Moooom: *Congrats, Marcus!*
Marcus: *Thank you!*
Moooom: *Knew you'd do it!*
Marcus: *Didn't expect to have my own space in under two weeks.*
Christy-Anne: *DE-COR-ATE, butthead.*

Charlene: *Please listen to her.*
Daaaad: *Did you at least put a sheet on your bedroom window like I said?*
Marcus: *I live in the Village, it's a free show. At 7 and 7 every day!*
Moooom: *Marcus Chastain!*
Charlene: *I'm sending you curtains and a rod.*
Marcus: *There are plenty of rods in the Village*
Christy-Anne: *Whoa!*
Charlene: *Wow!*
Daaaad: *TMI, Son!*
Moooom: *...and now I need brain bleach. [crying]*

I chuckled. My parents weren't all that shocked at my text. They were unbelievably supportive of me, and could be just as rough and tumble as me and my sisters. It was all in fun with us.

Christ, I loved my family.

Tucking away my cell phone, I headed to the door and grabbed the assignments someone had dropped off. I was going to take a cue from Sorcha and set up a white board on the outside of the room, so no one had to ask where their pieces were and wreck my concentration when they knocked.

There would be shopping tonight at the business supply store. I had a burning desire to go at lunch, but I wasn't going to reschedule with Ashton for *business supplies*.

Shuffling the papers, I sat down at the desk. I had to do some adjusting to the room before I could get going on the first assignment. This was my office and I wanted to set it up the way I liked.

My office.

That sounded amazing.

ASHTON WAS possibly the least compatible person I'd ever taken out on a date.

Twinky was one thing. Fun was another.

Ashton was *a whole other ball game.*

He was the guy in the room that had to let everyone know he was gay. He affected the lisp, the wrist, the giggle, the hip twitch. His speech was peppered with 'honey,' 'sweetie,' 'darling.' I was shocked he didn't just come right out and yell "yas, queen!" when I mentioned the studio I'd just been assigned.

Ashton was the kind of gay that I could only compare to a fire and brimstone southern evangelist preacher, screaming about Jesus and trying to convert everyone. Thumping the Bible, screaming about sin.

If Jesus was a Ferragamo-Loafer, Brioni High-sheen two piece suit, pale blue shirt with salmon silk cravat wearing gay man.

And Vogue was the Bible.

I was far from closeted. I had been brought up to believe there was nothing wrong with me. But I had also been brought up to know when to let my inner gay man out, and when not to. To know the kind of people I wanted to be surrounded by, and make sure that they were there for me and not for what I could get them or give them.

Apparently, Ashton hadn't had a single one of those lessons. Or, maybe he did and didn't care.

I'd heard the disgusted sighs of the people at other tables while we were eating. It was easy to tell that they weren't because we were a gay couple.

They were sighing because Ashton was *so fucking loud*.

He giggled and leaned forward, sipping his third or fourth lunch mojito. I lost track of the mojitos when he tossed in a Lemon Drop and California Sunrise.

"So, do you have a lot to do at work this afternoon?"

"Not much, but I wanted to get some stuff set up—"

"Let's pop over to my place." He grinned. Finally, he dropped his voice. "I'd like to see if the tight end has all the right kind of on-field skills."

And that was another mistake I'd made. It had just slipped out when we were discussing our younger lives. And despite the fact that I had been a wide receiver, and occasionally a center, he just liked to say *tight end*.

"Ashton—"

"Come on, come back with me. It doesn't have to be anything but a good fuck."

"No, Ashton. I'm risking my job."

"Then let's use your—"

"This date is over, Ash," I said, tossing the napkin on the table. "We're not looking for the same thing, at all, and this needs to end right now. I can't handle this."

"Ugh!" He dropped back into his chair. "Of course you can't handle me, no one can handle me."

"Including yourself, Ash," I said.

Standing, I pulled my wallet out of my pocket and pulled out two twenties. "That should cover my food and a generous tip. I mean, thanks for the restaurant rec, but I've got to come back when not everyone in here wants to take your head off with a meat cleaver." I turned and headed for the door.

"Why on Earth would they want to do that?" he gasped, indignant.

I turned back. "Because you're loud. You're annoying. You're pissing everyone else off with your free lunch show, when all they want is soup and salad in peace! Grow the hell up and stop acting a fool."

"I'm gay, this is just the way—"

Slamming my hands on the table, I leaned in and backed him down. "I'm gay, too, and you don't see me pissing off everyone else in the place. It's not your sexuality, Ashton. It's your rotten, narcissistic attitude. Grow. Up."

"Uh!" Ashton rolled his eyes. "I guess all you were was a hot ass."

I couldn't stop myself.

I turned, slapped my ass and stared right at him. "Honey, this is the hottest ass you are *never* going to tap. Say goodbye and give it a kiss."

Heading for the door, I realized everyone in the restaurant, including the waitstaff and two sous chefs peeking out from the back, was clapping. Stopping at the door, I let my inner actor out, and took a bow.

The isolation of my soundproof office was everything I needed when I finally got there. I'd stopped for a six pack of beer on the way there, because I sure as hell was going to need it that night.

Sorcha, however, was standing at her door as I walked by. "How'd it go?"

I held up the six pack of Brooklyn Brown Ale.

"Oh, shit, that good or that bad?"

"Bad. Terrible? No, let's go with horrific."

"I'm sorry, man," she said.

"Yeah, me too. I'm just gonna work on my assignments for the day and go to the office supply tonight for my fun stuff. That'll help. And then I'll go home and drink a few a beers with the best Chinese I've ever had."

She agreed, "That's a plan."

Charlene: DATE. Need info, pronto, lil bro!
Christy-Anne: DATE!?
Daaaad: It's June third.
Moooom: Martin! Quit it. Your son had a date.
Daaaad: Date!
Marcus: You are all intolerable and embarrassing.
Christy-Anne: Embarrassed? It's a group text and I used to give you wedgies in person. Spill it, M.
Marcus: It was horrible. I'm glad he works for a client and not in house.
Charlene: Was he cute?

Marcus: *I wouldn't have agreed to go with him if I didn't find him attractive, but OMG. I'm shocked the tablecloth didn't catch fire.*

Charlene: *Get lucky?*

Marcus: *Char!*

Moooom: *Charlene Elizabeth!*

Daaaad: *Charlene!*

Christy-Anne: *Did you?*

Marcus: *Lucky to get away, yes.*

Charlene: *Whomp whomp.*

Marcus: *I had to Make A Scene in the restaurant to get him to back off. It was just bad, you guys.*

Moooom: *Do you want us to come down? We could help with those curtains while we were there.*

Marcus: *I'm fine. I promise.*

Moooom: *You let us know if you need anything, Marc.*

Marcus: *I know, Mom. Thanks.*

I stopped in the hall and cocked my head.

Shit. I could hear Pollux barking from here. What was that fool dog up to? He'd never barked like this back at my parents' place. The only thing in the building that were a threat were probably the other tenants and some mice.

Okay, and a roach or five.

I walked up the stairs, and there was another note.

302,

Please, I'm begging you. Do something about your dog. I don't want to lodge a complaint with the owner. But I need to sleep and Poochie just keeps on keepin' on. He's also bothering Mrs. Benevedes downstairs, and she's eighty-nine and has had enough of life's shit already.

301

This was really a problem. I couldn't lose this place. I'd gotten such a deal on it and it gave me the freedom to not have to share with two or three other guys. I glanced at the bottom and it was a picture of someone angrily dialing a phone with their hat on backward.

I was suddenly aware of two things: One my neighbor was a dude, not a woman. And two...

Two, he was a Cubs fan.

A Cubs fan in New York City? I was enough of an outlier by being one in Troy, but this was the city that two of every sports team: football, baseball, basketball—and three local hockey teams...but did the Islanders ever really count?

I stared at the baseball cap.

Now, this was even worse. My dog was alienating a potential ally in this city. Being Cubs fans in Mets/Yankees territory was always a dangerous proposition. Not as dangerous as being a BoSox fan, but still a risky proposition. If I could find someone to watch a game with me once in a while, this would be a major, major win.

Shit. *Shit.*

I ran into my apartment and found Pollux on the couch, quite literally barking at the wall.

What was going on with this animal?

"Get down. Pollux, get down. Stop barking at the wall, you dingbat. It's a wall, you've seen them before!" I pulled him off the couch and put him on the ground. "You've walked into them!"

"Woof?" He cocked his head at me and I let out a sigh. Half basset hound, half golden retriever, all idiot.

I had to walk him, soon. I hadn't ordered the emergency potty patch yet, so he had to go out. But I wanted to get the next note up and call a truce. *Maybe* if he met Pollux, the idiot would stop barking at his wall.

I grabbed the pen and paper and wrote up a quick note, and as fast and as neat as I could, I sketched out a simple drawing offering an apology and the potential to make peace with me and the Wall Barking Wunderhund.

Pollux was nearly dancing in front of the door by the time I got done and he pulled hard on the leash as I headed for the bulletin board. He made a beeline for the stairs, but I stopped him just long enough to pin the note. He pulled so hard I thought I was going to go ass over teakettle down them before I could get him to heel.

"Dude, stop! I know you have to pee! You wouldn't be in a rush if you didn't bark at walls!"

He made it to the fire hydrant, thank God. I was afraid he was going to pee on the steps. The grocery store manager was outside hosing off the front of his place and I asked if I could borrow the hose.

"I wash. I watch so many dog peess on hydrant, I wash every day."

"Thank you! He doesn't usually make that a habit."

He waved me off. "You have good dog. No worries friend. At least you not drop a turd in front of my fruits and pretend you not see it."

I grimaced. "Ew."

"Very much ew. That is why we wash!"

Laughing, I headed down the block to the cross street and up to Washington Park. Apparently, Pollux had been pregaming and peed on every tree along the way, and on the way back. He was such a funny, friendly looking dog that people always wanted to make friends with him. Once around the park, though, and I was ready to go back.

I really just wanted to sit down, eat dinner on the couch and try relaxing a bit. The Brooklyn Brown Ale was calling my name.

CHAPTER FIVE

CHASE

MISTER ABRAMOVICH WAS HOSING the hydrant again. I was glad that he was—there were some nasty people in this city. I waved and walked into the bodega, heading for the vegetables and meats.

I stood staring at them for a minute, trying to figure out what I felt like cooking, if I felt like cooking and what the hell to cook.

Living next door to Abramovich and Daughter was the best thing ever. I rarely kept more than a day's worth of food in the house because they were right there, and everything was fresh. I cooked almost every night. Noah had laughed that I shopped every day, but when we compared our spending and our food waste, he was sold and found a great little bodega by his place.

I didn't want anything complicated, so I grabbed

a head of lettuce, a package of bacon, a cucumber and called it lettuce wedge salad kind of night.

Heading back out of the store, I danced around the hose that Mr. Abramovich was using, and swearing at. Apparently another dog owner had let their precious crap in front of his apples. Just from listening to him, I had picked up the words *stupid motherfuckers* in Russian, and he was using it liberally now.

Kieran had accidentally fallen asleep on the couch the night before and fled in a panic in the morning. We'd teasingly texted each other all day and immediately saw that while Kieran wasn't going to be a love interest, he was going to be a real friend. And that was worth the time I'd invested getting to know him. I'd already invited him to the bar on Thursday.

> **Kieran**: *It wasn't even a walk of shame, it was a flat out run of horror. I'm just getting home now and ohdearGod, I need a shower.*

I laughed at the text as I walked up the stairs. Yeah, this guy was going to be a winner in the friends department.

The giant green 301 on the bulletin caught my attention, and I stopped to pluck the new note off the board.

Last night had been the worst night yet for all the barking. And barking. And barking. I had determined that after the first morning note had disappeared, the situation had warranted a second note. This dog just could not keep barking overnight.

Even the sweet retiree the floor below had said something to me about Barky McBarkerson.

Depositing everything in the kitchen, I took a moment to turn on the oven to cook the bacon for my bacon crumbles. I dropped the note on the table and decided the shower that I also needed would wait until closer to bedtime.

I stared at the note again.

I liked animals. I did. They were wonderful. But in close quarters like this, where the buildings were old, and the walls weren't insulated or soundproofed...dogs had to not bark. Even if it was my own dog. Even it was the most adorable or awkward pup ever.

Snatching the paper back, I flipped it open.

301

I think my dog is broken. I have no idea why he barks at the walls. But what if we call a truce? There's a chance that this moron may just be barking because he doesn't know you. Meet him? And enjoy a beer with me over an afternoon of Cubbies baseball?

302

If I could have gasped, I would. I couldn't though because I was breathless.

A Cubbies fan? Next door? My eyes shot to the hat I had perched up on a shelf in the living room. It sat between two trophies, above a few ribbons and next to a single framed ticket.

It wasn't that I was even a hard-core Cubbies fan, it had grown more and more casual over the years. It was that I had so much attached to those memories.

Glancing back to the paper, there was an adorable but strange looking dog drawn on the bottom, with a case of Brooklyn Brown in his mouth, and a question on his face.

How could I say no? Maybe, just maybe, meeting the barking menace would solve the problem. And the idea of having an afternoon of baseball, beer, and maybe food would be amazing.

The hall outside the apartment was suddenly a racket. I heard a dog barking, but not toward the direction of me or the stairs. There were more bangs and swearing and someone yelled 'ouch' in the midst of the chaos.

The front door slammed and I could swear that I heard the glass crack.

I ran for my apartment door, slamming my keys in my pocket and jerking the door shut behind me. I nearly flew down the flight from the third floor to the second. As soon as I was at the top of the next flight, I could see what was going on.

A very large, broad shouldered brown haired man had a greasy looking dude in a headlock. Missy Billing was standing back against the wall, holding a hand to her face, clearly bleeding. A dog was barking and growling at the large man and his quarry.

I jumped down the last stairs.

"Lemme go!"

"Give me the wallet, you asswipe. Give it to me!"

Missy looked confused watching this, so I opted to run over to her—not to mention Burly Man had the grease ball in hand. "Missy?"

"Oh, shit, Chase, thank God!"

"What's going on?"

She glanced at the two men fighting. "They came out of nowhere and slammed into the wall next to me."

The burly guy slammed his fist into the greasy one's neck and finally, Grease Ball let go and slumped to the floor.

Burly Man stood, and revealed a very delicious looking human. Tall, but leanly muscled, and his sleeves were rolled up which did funny things to me.

Glancing around, he finally spied the dog and lunged for the leash. "Pollux, quit it. You can pee on him if you want, but you're not allowed to kill him." He found me standing next to Missy and seemed to hiccup, then held the leash out for me. "Can you hold him for a minute?"

Mute, I nodded and held the dog who was now more interested in me. The man leaned down and flipped the unconscious grease ball over and yanked something out of his front pants pocket.

Coming back over to me and Missy, he held the objects out. "Here you go. Wallet and keys."

"*Holy shit*, he pickpocketed me?" Missy stared at the wallet.

"I've seen him around, I think it was more nefarious than that. I think he planned to rob your apartment."

I had already dialed 911 on the phone, but was rendered speechless by that assessment.

"Hello? This is 911, what is your emergency?"

"Oh! Yeah, my neighbor was just attacked and pickpocketed. We have the guy, he's knocked out. Could you send police and an ambulance?"

"What's your address, sir?"

I rattled it off and the operator asked if I wanted to stay on the line, but I didn't think it was really necessary. I thought that I heard a cop car screaming closer already.

The greasy dude groaned from the ground and the Burly Hunk Man stood over him, beckoning for the leash for his dog. I handed it over, and he nodded.

"Pollux, sit." He looked at the guy who was starting to rouse. "He's not a bad dog, but he knows s-i-c, and I suggest you don't move."

The guy tried to raise his head, but flopped back down to the ground with a thump.

"Missy, are you okay?" I asked.

She looked at me, and finally seemed to come back to herself. "Yes. Yeah. I'm fine. Holy shit. I'm good. I had no idea the guy had pickpocketed me. Thank you..."

"Marcus," the handsome burly man supplied. "Don't mention it."

The cops hopped up the steps at that moment and quickly assessed the situation. They waited for the ambulance before moving the grease ball, but took statements from me, Missy, and Marcus.

It turned out that Marcus had been walking a few dozen feet behind Missy on the way to the building. He'd seen the guy around and hadn't liked his look much, and when he saw the hand dip into her purse as she turned to walk up the stairs, he'd gone full linebacker and slammed him to the door as it closed behind Missy.

He'd managed to tackle and wrestle him into the hall and that was when I came flying down the stairs.

We watched as the medics rolled the handcuffed suspect out the door on a stretcher. He'd had a pretty good cut on this forehead and they wanted to check him for a concussion.

As soon as the door closed, the officer turned to us. "Well, sir, you'll be delighted to know that there has been a rash of break-ins in the area and we've been trying to figure how it was happening. It looks like you just solved the whole thing."

"Good," Marcus said. "Glad I could help."

The officer turned to Missy. "I'd ask the super to change your locks and maybe get a keypad for the front door as well. The latch didn't catch well and that's how you were able to fall into the building."

"I'll talk to the owner," I volunteered.

"I'll stop buy the hardware store and grab a new lock set for Missy's door. I can put it in tomorrow."

Missy nodded. "Thank you, I'd appreciate that." She knelt down to the dog. "And thank you, Pollux. You're a good boy, aren't you? Going after the bad guys."

He woofed, and then gave three sharp barks I was entirely to familiar with.

My head snapped up to Marcus. "You're three-oh-two!"

"Uh, yeah?"

"I'm three-oh-one!"

"Ohhh, yeah... Uh..." He rubbed his neck and looked down.

"You're a Cubs fan." The words were out of my mouth before I could stop them.

"I am?"

"Are you not sure?

"I'm not sure where this is going..."

I laughed. "I'm a Cubs fan."

"Oh. Oh! You are? Wait, you noticed the Cubs hat in my drawing?"

Nodding, I couldn't keep the idiotic smile off my

face. "I'm a graphic designer. Details like that jump out at me all the time. I'm surprised you noticed the one in mine..."

Marcus was clearly shocked. "Well, I uh...I guess my idea of you meeting Pollux here has been accomplished."

Missy leaned in between us. "The nice officer said we're free to go now, so I'm going to let you two guys chat it up in the hall."

"Oh, hey, sorry," I said, kicking myself mentally for ignoring the woman who was attacked half an hour before. "Yeah, I'll go talk to Mister Davos about this front door."

"Thank you," she said, sincerely. "Thank you both. That could have been a real mess if you hadn't been on your toes, Marcus."

"Pollux growled at him the other day. And I already didn't like the guy." He smiled. "Anyone would have done the same thing."

Missy patted his cheek, and grinned at me. "Newb to the city. Chase, just make sure that he knows anyone wouldn't have done that. Just a cute former football player from Troy."

Marcus's cheeks went utterly pink, and it was one of the cutest things I'd seen in ages. He affected a terrible southern accent for his answer. "Well, schucks, Missy. T'weren't no theng. You're right welcome."

Her laughter floated back at us as she ascended the stairs to her apartment. "Thanks, guys!"

Marcus looked lost a moment later. "So, I have to apologize for my idiot dog. I don't know why he's so keen on barking at the wall. He's actually a really good dog and I don't want anyone upset with him."

"Well, he's met me now," I said, crouching down

to give him some ear scratches. "Maybe now he'll relax a bit at night."

"I sure hope so," Marcus said. "I like this building and you've all been really nice to me since I moved in."

"Except for poochy here, we're all reasonably pleased with you too. The old guy who lived there was a crab and a jerk and used to make nasty sexist comments to Missy. I had to defend her more than once. And the homophobic comments..."

God, the times I had held my tongue against that asshole and his comments. We were in the Village. Gay was not a new thing here, and that old man couldn't stand that some of us liked dick.

"I'm happy to replace his homophobia with homophilia." Marcus laughed.

Wait.

What?

CHAPTER SIX

MARCUS

ONCE AGAIN, MY SHOCKING ABILITY with words rushed to the forefront and I outed myself.

I figured this Chase guy was at least an ally, if he was bitching about a homophobe. So, I had that going for me, but still. I knew better. I'd learned the hard way that not everyone was okay with gay men. They might even be fine with lesbians, but men with men freaked them out.

Thanks, toxic masculinity!

Chase didn't seem to react to my outing myself, still petting Pollux. I just let it go. Either he was or wasn't an ally and that was that.

"So, how about if we let Pollux stiff around my place," Chase said. "If you think that would reinforce that I'm the good guy and not here to steal his bed."

Okay, he was cool with this. "Yeah, I mean, that sounds like the right thing to do."

"Good," Chase said, and stood up. "Let's go."

He held his hand out and I froze. Why was he holding his hand out? Was I supposed to take it? Slap it? High five? Lace our fingers together?

Pollux barked.

I was an asshole. He wanted the leash.

Jerking myself back to the real world, I offered it and he took it with a smile. I watched as he headed up the stairs with my dog.

And a very, very hot ass.

Shit.

I trotted up the stairs after him to the third floor, and he went right to his door. He popped the door open, clearly having left it unlocked on his flight down, and Pollux trotted in happily.

Pulling the door closed, I realized his apartment was a quarter turn off of mine, meaning my living room was against his bedroom.

That's why he could hear my idiot dog so well.

"Man, I didn't realize they did that," I mumbled. "Logically, this building should be mirrored, and that should be your living room."

"Nothing in this building is logical," Chase said. "Absolutely nothing." He leaned down and unclipped Pollux's leash. "Go crazy, my canine friend. Make sure you sniff everything and get used to me. Because I want to sleep in my bedroom."

Pollux trotted happily around the room, sniffing anything and everything.

"Would you like a beer? Soda?"

"Oh, uh...just a soda, thanks."

I followed him into the kitchen, where I saw my drawing on the table. I picked it up and smirked. I was impressed he had noticed that Cubs hat I put on the dog.

"So you really are a Cubs fan?"

Chase pointed back to the living room, and I saw the shelf there with the Cubs paraphernalia. Hat, tickets, bobble heads, trophies, and a picture.

"I am a light fan, now," he said. "I used to be bigger into it. But...things change, and I can't really dedicate the time or mental bandwidth to it. I just roll along with the scores online."

"Well, that's not nearly as much fun as a game," I said.

"No, but like I said, it's not really something I can find the time for."

There was more to it than I was entitled to know at the moment. Chase handed me the soda.

"So, do you think Poochy—"

"Pollux." I laughed.

"Pollux," he corrected, "will be less barky now that he's had the run of the place and knows I'm over here?"

"Well, here's hoping," I said, and raised my can to toast the idea.

"Prost," he answered, and tapped his drink against mine. "I will give you this. Your dog is adorable. But um...what the hell is he?"

"Half basset hound and half golden retriever," I answered, laughing. "Aunt Bits forgot to get her golden snipped and he made moves on the neighbor's prize bitch. Pollux, his two sisters, and compensation to the tune of three thousand dollars were the result."

"What? Why?"

"Because the pregnancy didn't result in pure bassett hounds, so the neighbor said she could either give him the money or they'd go to civil court."

"Over a dog being a dog?"

"Bassett hound puppies go for a thousand dollars apiece, and a breeder like Mister Haywood isn't a backyard breeder or a puppy mill. He's a very reputable breeder, and Bits was happy to pay it because it was her fault." I tipped my head, considering things. "She also had to home the puppies, and I fell for this dumbass."

Pollux trotted in, sniffing things as he went. Chase bent down after putting his beer on the table. "You are a cute thing, aren't you?"

He was enamored with the dog, to be sure. And I couldn't help finding myself a little enamored with him.

Christ, he was going to end up being straight.

Chase was standing outside his door the next morning in a robe and holding a steaming cup of coffee. He looked like hell.

"Oh, no," I murmured. "Really? All night again?"

"All night. All effing night."

I didn't know what to say. There was no way Pollux could stay with me if he was going to bark all night long.

"Chase, man...I don't know what to say..."

"You'll be in here tonight, at seven, with my friends helping me switch the living room and bedroom."

"Are you sure—"

He pushed the door open. "I'm not as big of a dick that I'm going to make you get rid of your dog. The rooms are the same size. Just show up and pay for pizza and beer."

"Done, man," I said, sticking my hand out. "Thank you for not suggesting—"

He gripped my hand. "Stop right there. He's a dog. I'm a human. I can adapt better than he can. Plus, he helped with Missy yesterday so there's no apologies necessary."

"Thanks," I answered, not letting go of his hand right away. His hand was warm and soft, and oddly comfortable in my own. Had we not shook hands last night? Why did I not remember the way it felt.

He was straight. That was why. I pulled my hand back and I could see confusion on his face as he stared at his hand.

Shit, was he *questioning*?

Chase lifted his eyebrows and sighed. "Okay. Seven. Don't be late. I need my beauty sleep, otherwise," his hand swept the tableau of himself, "you can see what I look like."

Hot? Sexy? Alluring in that robe with those long, muscular legs sticking out? Even his feet were sexy? "I get it," I finally said. "I'm also going to set up a recorder and see if we can catch some kind of noise at night making him crazy. He didn't do this for the first week I was here, so I'm wondering if it's something else."

"Good idea," Chase yawned. "I'm going to get ready for work. I'll drag my friends back. See you tonight."

He pushed the door in and disappeared.

I looked down at my dog. "You. I don't know what to do with you. It's a wall, you furry asshole. Stop barking at it like it's in your way. The only time you've ever paid attention to any walls was when you walked smacked into them."

I only did once around the block with Pollux before I had to run off to get to the studio. I had four more projects in the mailbox, and I trotted into the room studying them. Two were marked rush but had no deadline. The other two had deadlines in three weeks. Plus the ones I already had that were urgent...

I grabbed the phone and dial my manager's number.

"Liggit." His tone was clipped.

"Hey, Jerry, it's Marcus. I have two assignments here marked urgent and have no date on them. How would I find out about those."

"Two?" I heard him shuffling paperwork. "That's weird. There was supposed to be numbers on those. Vi! Where's the urgent sheet?"

He screamed right in my ear and I wanted to laugh. Screaming into a sound engineer's ear was kind of a stupid move since we relied on our hearing for work.

There was a rustling of papers, and I shook my

head. Everything else was done by computer and spreadsheet, except the urgents? That was down right ridiculous. Someone slapped a paper on a surface.

"Here we go," Jerry said, "Thanks, Vi."

"Get organized, jackhole," Vi snapped into the phone.

"So what are the numbers?"

I rattled off the two I had gotten today and the two yesterday. "I need those dates to—"

"Oh, fuck," he hissed.

"Oh fuck what?"

I could hear him hiss between his teeth. "All four of those are Roberts' pieces. They need to be done today."

Ed Roberts strikes again. "Jerry, there's ten hours of audio between the four assignments. I can't do that all today. I have—"

"Roberts requested you, the one who assisted Sorcha on the last set. He really likes your style, and he wanted to rerecord some stuff he didn't like with the last tech."

Shit.

Shit shit shit.

"I can't even get ten hours today. Give me a priority, please, Jerry."

"The two yesterday were new requests. The two today are revisions."

"That helps a lot, man, thank you. I cannot possibly get these done today, but I will get as much of the revisions done as I can. Hopefully both."

"Roberts isn't going to be happy."

"Neither is my neighbor whom I owe a *big fucking favor* to for not making me get rid of my dog," I snapped. "So he can wait. Because now I have to apologize to the hottie next door that I can't be there tonight to help rearrange his whole apartment to accommodate my idiot wall-barking canine."

There was silence on the phone, and then. "Okay. I'll let him know."

"Thank you."

I placed the receiver down quietly, turned, and punched the wall.

CHAPTER SEVEN

CHASE

MARCUS302: *DUDE. I am SO sorry.*
Marcus302: *I got slammed at work and I'm going to be here until probably eight or later.*
Marcus302: *Don't hate me. Or my dog. I'll still pay for beer and pizza. Just tell me when you want it and I'll have it all delivered.*

I knew he didn't want to blow me off. He felt so bad about Pollux barking all night. He seemed like the kind of guy who wanted to make everything right.

Chaser: *Don't worry about the beer and pizza. Find another way to make it up to me. We'll be done in an hour anyway.*

I was sad though. He seemed like a really nice guy who just wanted to be a nice neighbor. I was happy to have anything aside from Veteran Homophobe next door.

There was no way of knowing how many times I had told that man he was living in the goddamn Greenwich Village. The place practically invented gay. There were the Stonewall Riots, and one of the oldest Pride Parades I knew of. And the old badger wouldn't even hear it.

"Real men don't fuck other men."

The words had boiled around my brain, time and again. He always hissed and spit at gay couples. Not just any gay couples though. The ladies were exempt. He seemed to like those, and I'd nearly punched him the one time I caught him watching a couple across the street make out hot in heavy in their window.

I was shocked he didn't just whip it out and masturbate.

I'd told the ladies what had happened, and their windows were never opened again. Until, the day his family had moved him out of the apartment and into an assisted living facility, closer to them in Staten Island.

I'd almost thrown a party.

In fact, the whole block had almost thrown a party. Mister Abramovich was delighted because he knew the old fart's dog was one of the ones who *sheet in front of my dragon fruit*. On a regular basis.

Marcus302: *Could you do me a tremendous favor and I will keep you in pizza and beer for months?*

Chaser: *Dog?*
Marcus302: *Please?*
Chaser: *Who has the key.*
Marcus302: *Missy has one.*
Marcus302: *Thank you thank you thank you thank you. Thank you. Thaaaaank you.*

Marcus was lucky I liked the wall-barking moron.

Missy was able to give me the key at six and Pollux was practically dancing by the time I got him on the leash and down the stairs. He went straight for the hydrant and Mister Abramovich raised his eyebrow at me as Pollux relieved himself.

"This is not your dog?"

"No, sorry about the pee."

"This is the other boy's dog."

"He got stuck at work."

"Ah, so you help him out with the dog. Very good."

Pollux trotted away from the hydrant and Mr. Abramovich hosed it off immediately.

"I'm really sorry—"

"Dogs pee, my friend. I wash this every day. You are good man for helping the other with the dog." He nodded me onward, and Pollux seemed to know we were dismissed.

We headed halfway around Washington Square when I realized I really had to get home and the dog was romancing other dogs and bushes in equal amounts. He'd been done peeing for half the time. I cut through the park, and headed back to the apartment.

The irony of me walking the very beast that was making me rearrange my whole apartment was not lost on me. Ushering him back in the apartment, I realized I had to feed and water Pollux too.

I filled his water bowl and he went to town on it, and quickly found the food and food bowl. I didn't know how much to give him, so I guessed. It made a disgusting noise into the dish, and smelled like hell. But he apparently had no issue with it and chowed down.

Looking around, waiting for the dog to finish his meal, I realized there wasn't much to the place. It looked very much like he'd gone to Ikea for three basic things: a table and chairs, a couch, and probably a bed.

I hoped he wasn't living on the edge of broke. I hated when people had to do that. But, it was more likely he just hadn't had a chance to really settle in.

Except for the pictures.

The one wall of the living room was covered in framed pictures from top to bottom. I glanced at Pollux who was still busy with his food, then walked over to the wall of images.

I could see Marcus in a lot of them, at all ages. PeeWee football, kindergarten graduation, a second birthday picture. More of him with a family; mother, father, two sisters. Vacations, pets, biking, school plays, more football. There was one that looked like it had been snapped the weekend of his going away party, and a few Cubs games with either his dad or the whole family.

It was genuine Americana.

It was also a shot through my heart.

This guy's family fucking *loved* him. They didn't care if he was gay, which was probably why he blurted out that he was. Even in a small city like Troy, New York—information gleaned from one of the photos—there were enough homophobes to make a person shy if your family wasn't 100 percent behind you.

Marcus clearly had that.

I perused the images a little more and stopped dead on a medium frame at the end. There was a framed medal, and a picture of Marcus, standing with about a dozen other people wearing the medals with the giant "A" on them. A little plaque too.

Marcus Chastain
Best Male Audiobook Narrator

Oh. My. Fucking. God.

I had *masturbated* to this man's voice.

This man brought the most delicious fantasies to life on my audio player. It wasn't an easy task—being demi, getting off was a trick sometimes. Rereading a book I liked several times helped me get to know the characters and forge a connection with them. I had a small collection of favorites, and then I'd discovered audiobooks.

Specifically, Marcus Chastain's audiobooks.

Just the memory of his silky tones through the headset as I listened to one of my favorite gay romances—for the tenth or twentieth time—had me half hard against my zipper.

Shocked I'd kept my eyes in my head and my dick in my pants, I looked at the dog in the doorway.

"Jesus Christ."

Running into the kitchen, I quickly filled the water and bowl, where Pollux was happy to occupy himself. I made sure the living room light was on, the doors closed and—locking the door—made a mad dash the ten feet to my apartment door and slammed it.

Marcus Chastain lived across the landing from me.

Fuck.

How had I not recognized his voice? I listened to those books at least once a week, and I didn't recognize him!

Because he wasn't whispering about stretching your pretty hole to fit his cock and tempting me with slick fingers over mine.

Holy crap on a cracker, the fly of my pants was making impressions on my dick. This was bad. This was really bad. My neighbor had one of the sexiest voices on the damn planet and now all I was going to do was strain to hear that when he was in the room with me.

I thumped my head back against the door.

Doomed. *Dooooooooomed.*

Taking several long, slow breaths, I managed to calm my heart rate and get my erection to deflate. I could not be caught with that kind of *affliction* when my friends came over to help me move rooms.

It was probably better that I was moving my bed away from his living room wall.

Less chance of him hearing me furiously jerk off to one of his books.

Oh, God.

KIERAN LOOKED between Noah and Uriah and back again. I tried not to laugh. Jace wasn't so lucky, and Vin fell in right behind him.

"You've never seen identical twins before?" they chorused.

Kieran burst out laughing with Jace and Vin. "You did that on purpose."

"Of course, we did," they spoke together again.

"I like to call them Tomax and Xamot," Maddox said, gesturing with his beer. "They do that creepy twin shit all the time."

I could also see that Kieran was utterly star struck with Maddox sitting there on the edge of my couch. To us, he was just Madd, but to the rest of the world, he was Maddox Jones, the lead singer of Robot Servant. Currently, two songs on the charts and two gold records on his wall at home. He and the band were working on a new album that everyone was sure was going to go platinum.

I hoped it did. He deserved it after all he'd been through.

"I think the place turned out pretty well," Vin said. "It's a little weird to have to go into the kitchen through the bedroom, but at least the dog is further away."

"I might actually get a full night's sleep!" I clapped my hands in delight.

"That was very gay of you," Uriah deadpanned.

We all burst out laughing. Everyone in the room *was* gay or bi, with the exception of Maddox.

Vin put his beer down, and stood. "I have to be the party pooper, you guys. I have a tough case coming up and I need to prep. I need a metric ton of precedent to get my client cleared, and I'm behind."

"Ha, you said prep." Noah giggled.

Vin rolled his eyes. "Yeah, this one is figuratively being screwed in the ass. I feel for this woman. I wish we had the resources of the other law team because what's going down isn't anywhere near right." He let out a sigh. "Anyway, attorney client privilege and all that. I got reading."

"Thanks for coming over, man," I said, walking him to the front door. "I really appreciate it."

"No biggie." He nodded. "Sleep is important and you're a nice guy for not making Butthead get rid of the dog."

"Dog's nice," I said.

"What about the butthead?"

"Stopped a mugger the other night," I answered with a shrug.

"Damn, so he's nice too. Well, I hope this solves a lot of the mess. Let me know if you need any help again. I'm always willing."

"That's why you're not a rich lawyer," I teased.

"Eh, I can sleep at night. Others can't for all their

money."

Giving him a hearty pat on the shoulder, I nodded. "Good man. Don't be a stranger."

"You either." He pulled the door shut behind himself.

I turned to find the rest of the guys were cleaning up the mess and getting ready to go. I was relieved I was going to be able to sleep finally, and that all of my friends had the good sense at this stage of life that staying here and drinking ourselves stupid wasn't really a good plan.

Jace, I noticed, hung back.

The rest—Noah, Uriah, Madd, and Kieran—all performed their ritual goodbye and were out the door and down the stairs in just a few minutes.

"Need a couch, Jace?" I asked, watching him wipe the coffee table.

"Do you mind?"

"Who is it this time?"

He sighed. "Silas. Took my credit card. Ran it up, and pretended to be me, closed it and laughed in my face when I couldn't get the company to believe it wasn't me."

I raised an eyebrow.

"They dropped the charges but refused to open it again. So now I get to pay on it, and have no place to charge the things I need. Like food."

I shook my head. "You need to get the hell out of that apartment, man. All the way out. Why don't you double up with one of us? I mean, I'm only asking for rental of the couch if you stay."

"I can't do that..."

"Your pride is going to be your downfall, Jace. We're all here for you." He was about to start arguing with me, but I held up my hand. "No, I know. The couch is yours tonight if you can deal with Fido. Shower and fridge too. Anything you like."

"I do..." He coughed. "I wanted to ask you for one favor. And it kills me to do this. But could you co-sign a safety deposit box with me? I don't trust these assholes to keep their mitts off my stuff, and I want to keep things like my birth certificate and important docs away from them."

"Why co-sign?"

"Because if something happens—"

"Have they threatened you?" My overprotective mama bear came out and I drew up taller.

"No, no, nothing like that. I'm just worried."

"Are you sleeping on your backpack again?"

"I have to," he whispered.

I was going to have to talk to the others about this. Jace struggled too much and he was too proud to ask for help. We were going to have to force it on him. "We can pop over to the bank tomorrow and open one."

His relief was palpable. "Thanks, man."

"Meanwhile, shower's free here whenever you want to get away from those assholes."

"Appreciate it." He grinned, heading back that way. "I don't want to walk onto the set and stink."

Shaking my head, I sighed. The set. An underpaid camera man at a bad studio in Queens that produced nothing but stilted news and cheap, air-able smut for cishet men who were stuck in the throes of toxic masculinity.

I wondered if they even knew that Jace was gay.

I hoped not, for his sake.

Just as I was about to retreat to my new bedroom, my phone rang in my pocket. Confused, I pulled it out and twisted my lips when I saw the name on the front.

Beth Garcia (Mom)

Tonight was not the night for this, and it took all I had not to swipe and send her to voice mail.

Swipe to answer. "Hello?"

"Chase, is that you?"

"Hi, Mom." I hoped the grimace I was making didn't sound through the phone.

"Hon, you know it's your dad's birthday this weekend."

"Yeah, I know." I sighed.

"Did you book your ticket?"

"I'm not coming."

"Chase—"

"Every year, Mom. For twelve years. You try to get me to go back there and every year I tell you no. I don't go to Bumblefuck, Indiana for any reason. At all. Not Christmas, not Arbor Day, not even my father's sixty-fifth birthday. I'm not welcome, and I'm not going to impose myself on people who don't want to be seen around the town faggot. So. No, I haven't booked my ticket. I'll send a fruit cake."

"Chase Martin. You have a shitty attitude."

The laughter boiled out of me, and I was unable—well, maybe unwilling—to stop it. "A broken zygomatic bone, a sprained shoulder, and busted steamer trunk on the way out the door makes me think that just maybe it's not *my* attitude that's shitty."

"Your brother—"

"Was the one who threw me out the door onto my steamer trunk while Auntie Maude was icing Hank's knuckles from breaking my eye socket! Give me a break, Mom. Just do everyone a favor and forget my number, okay? Send an email. That way I can ignore you at my leisure and you can still feel like you're trying."

"Chase—"

I swiped the connection closed. I missed angry hang ups from when I was kid. I realized I was unconsciously running a finger over the tiny scar next to my eye.

Taking a deep breath, I tried to center myself. I wasn't going home, I wasn't going to be guilted into going home. I left the day after I turned eighteen and who I was before was relegated to the shelf in the living room. Bedroom.

I was better than just being the Bumblefuck faggot.

I heard the shower go on, and I let out a breath. I had friends who needed me and wanted me around.

With a final, firm nod, I walked into to the kitchen to do—just about anything with my hands.

CHAPTER EIGHT

MARCUS

THE IDEA HIT ME OUT OF THE BLUE. I snapped my head up and grinned at the screen I had been staring at too long.

A baseball game.

I owed Chase *so much* after taking care of Pollux for me, and having ditched him completely. He rearranged his house to accommodate Pollux, and I had to back out.

I'd been stuck at work for three nights getting Roberts' pieces done, and then for the following two weeks, I'd been running late leaving because of a really bad commercial they were trying to save. Sorcha and I had found each other quite literally banging our head on our respective soundboards over the thing.

I found her singing a mantra as she did. "This sucks, this sucks, this sucks, this sucks."

"Does it suck?"

She looked up at me. "It feels like I'm in a vacuum pressure system and someone keeps flushing the toilet."

Pausing, I considered her words. "Impressive metaphor. And completely correct. Why does this suck so much? Why are we both dying slowly here?"

"The content, the product, the acting, the cinematography," she grumbled. "Honestly. It's like an eight year old produced this. Two weeks is too long for a thirty second spot."

"I think you're insulting eight year olds," I said. "I also think that the fact they keep sending us a new version of it we can't sync old sound to is a big factor."

She tapped a sheet of paper. "I have a damned spread sheet of the times for the sounds, and they *never sync*." She flipped the end of the paper over and it cascaded off the desk. "See? Every rework. Nothing the same."

I plunked into the chair. "We need to talk to Jerry about this contract. We need to put them on a finalized footage only rider from now on."

"Goddddd, yes," she moaned.

"Editing break. I need your opinion on something totally unrelatedly related."

"Was that phrase even allowed in the English language?"

"Don't care. I owe my neighbor big time. He rearranged his house to accommodate my dog, and now he's been walking him every night when he gets home so I don't go home to a pissed up house."

"Lord, man you do owe him."

"I think I came up with a way to pay him back. He has a little shrine to the Cubs in his living room. Bedroom. Whatever room that is now. And I was thinking, the Mets play the Cubs, and there's a three game series coming up next week."

"Get the man tickets, and take him to the game!"

Grinning, I nodded. "So you like the idea?"

"I think that's the perfect way to pay him back for all this dog walking."

"Good. That's what I'm doing then. We're going to see the Mets play the Cubs. I'll hop on the computer tonight and get the tickets."

She elbowed me in the side. "Get *good* ones, Marc. Really good ones if they're available."

"Oh, I know. Wait, you don't think I'm asking him on a date, do you? I don't think he's gay...I'm the only fool who outs themselves in the hallway."

"No, I'm not saying it's a date. I'm saying you need to get him good seats because you owe him. Big time."

I nodded. I did. It wouldn't hurt to get to know the guy who had the hot ass next door, either.

Straight. Don't go there.

Standing up, I grabbed her hand. "Come on. It's three-thirty on a Friday, and we're staring at another two hours of work each. Let's go find Jerry and talk to him about this. I don't want to be here any later than we have been."

"What's Jerry going to do? We have to finish these—"

I yanked her down the hall. "We're going to make him aware of how much time we're each putting into these damn things."

Jerry was sitting in his office, looking at his screen with his expression of deep concern. I knocked and walked in, but it took him a minute to look up.

"Hey, Marcus, Sorcha. Uh, are you two anywhere near done with your commercials? I have a backlog we need to tackle, and the delays on those are making me nervous."

"Well, we've been working on them," Sorcha said. "But they keep changing the finals. Not a lot, but—"

"Wait, what?" He sat up straight in his chair. "They're changing the finals? We have no change orders." He slammed his hand on the speaker. "Vi, do we have any change orders for the Brixton account?"

"You know we don't, Jerry," she huffed. "I just updated you this morning."

"Just making sure I heard right," he said. Jerry grabbed the phone and dialed an extension, motioning for us to just stay where we are. "Hardy, get up here."

Sorcha grimaced, and I tossed her a confused look. "Jimmy Hardison. Our data manager. He's a dinosaur." Her words were whispered.

A man not much older than either of us walked in and I shot Sorcha a withering look.

She chuckled. "In IT. I meant in IT."

"Yeah, sure," I mumbled.

Jerry either didn't hear us or ignored us. "Hardy, why have new files been uploaded to the server without a change order on my desk?"

"Huh?"

Jerry's fingers flew over his keyboard, and he pulled up the files Sorcha and I were working on. There were a dozen copies there, all labeled sequentially. "These are not supposed to be on our server. What are they doing there? You're the only one with access to upload, and it's never to be done without a CO."

"I got COs for those." He hip checked Jerry out of the way and pulled up a different file. Opening it, there were a dozen, matching COs in there.

I stabbed the screen. "I've only been here three weeks, but those are all DOCX files, and your COs, previous to this were PDF."

"Marcus is right," Sorcha said. "The COs only come down the pike as PDF because Jerry does them manually and scans them in so he knows what's going on."

Jerry fluttered his hand at her. "Exactly. You've been here for fifteen years, Hardy. Why the hell don't you know my system!"

He ran a hand down his face. "Fine. I let them upload because they said they sent the wrong file. I've been overwhelmed trying to keep this place organized on the back end and I didn't think that it was going to hurt anything if I let them."

"Fuck!" Jerry slammed his hand on the table. "They've been wandering through our system, Hardy?"

"Nah, no, I only let them upload—"

"You gave them access! If there was a person on their end worth their salt in IT, you gave them the key to the whole fucking system!"

"I've been overwhelmed—"

"Why didn't you ask me for help!"

"I..."

"Jesus, Hardy." He scrubbed his hand down his face. "We need to lock the whole system down, and transfer everything to a new internal server." He pointed at Hardy. "Hire someone to help you, you moron. Don't ever give anyone permission to upload again." He pointed at us. "The Brixton account is frozen. Fuck 'em. Forget 'em. Move on to the next thing tomorrow—Monday. Whatever."

"You got it," Sorcha said.

He plunked back into the chair. "Look, if anyone in this company is feeling overwhelmed I want you to come to me and ask for help. We're successful enough that if you're running to catch up, we probably have the resources to hire someone. Hardy, seriously. Find someone who can help you manage this."

Hardy looked devastated and relieved at the same time. "I don't know if I can find anyone fast enough to help me, boss. I'm out of the loop with new IT guys. I only know old grizzled dudes like me, who miss reel-to-reel and aren't convinced the Cloud is safe."

"We'll figure it out on Monday. Everyone go home. You've all done too much overtime this week as it is." He closed the top of the laptop he had on his desk. "Seriously. Go have a beer or whatever. I'll worry about all of this tomorrow. Hardy, just make sure you lock everyone out of the system who isn't an employee, eh?"

"You got it, Jerry." He nodded and walked back out of the room.

"That was nice of you not to fire him," Sorcha said.

"He's a good guy," Jerry said. "I just want you all to ask me for help if you think you need it. I'm not going to fire him for an old school practice of *grin and bear it.*"

I nodded. "That's very true. None of us should have to grin and bear it."

He tapped his nose, then pointed to the door. "Get out. Go home. Get drunk or something. Come back Monday. We'll start fresh."

Sorcha and I nodded together and headed out the door and back down to the studios. She clapped a hand on my shoulder. "Good job. I just assumed that Jerry had okayed all that."

"I did too, honestly, and I was going to complain about him blindly accepting change orders." I grinned. "I'm glad this was so much less nefarious than him doing a cash grab."

"I'm closing up and heading out. Hubby and I have a hot date with a cool drink on a roof top." She smiled. "Care to join us?"

"Your hot date? No, too straight."

She laughed. "Good point. When is that game you want to take your neighbor to?"

Looking at the face of my phone, I gasped. "Shit, it's this weekend! I need tickets!"

"Hop to it! And I'll see you Monday."

I nodded and ducked into my studio, and scrolling through the available tickets this weekend.

> **Marcus302**: *Hey, are you busy Sunday afternoon?*
> **Chaser**: *Uh, maybe why?*
> **Marcus302**: *I owe you, big time, for forgiving me for ditching you, for walking my dog, and for letting me keep him.*
> **Chaser**: *Just buy me a pizza.*
> **Marcus302**: *No. Bigger. Sunday afternoon?*
> **Chaser**: *Yeah, I'm free.*
> **Marcus302**: *Good. I'll be at your door at eleven.*
> **Chaser**: *That's not afternoon!*

AT ELEVEN in the morning, I knocked on Chase Garcia's door.

He opened it before the knock even died in the hallway.

Well.

I gave him a charming grin. "Good morning. Are you set and ready to go?"

He looked me up and down, shocked. "Are you...are you decked out in *Cubs* gear? Do you want to get shot?"

"Not particularly, but I'm not going to a Cubs game in *Mets* gear." I made a fake spitting sound.

Chase's eyes bugged right out of his head. "A *what*?"

"A Cubs game. There's a three game series, and I got us tickets for this afternoon's game. So, let's get going."

"I...uh." He looked down at himself, his eyes then darting around. "Hold on? I gotta change." He flew away from the door and back into his apartment. I laughed as he dove into the closet in the now living room and dug his way in.

Clicking the door closed, I looked around the former living room, waiting for him. His room was a fashion statement, with mute silvers and blues, pale gray furniture that was all reclaimed and refinished, and a set of gray and silver curtains on the windows.

Chase popped back into the bedroom and whipped his original shirt off and—

He was lithe and toned and his skin was a perfect tan color displaying his Latino heritage. A dusting of dark hair on his chest set off his skin, and it disappeared from his chest to just above his navel, where it picked back up and disappeared behind the waist of his pants.

Ah, shit.

I spun back to the door and flicked the chain for something to do.

Holy crap, Chase Garcia was a *god*.

Go away, erection. Go away. Bad timing.

"Ready?"

He was right at my shoulder, and I could feel the warmth of him radiating on my arm.

No! Bad dick! Back! Behave!

I nodded and pulled the door open, praying that

my one hundred and ninety dollar jeans were going to be able to contain my massive—amount of lust.

Chase pulled the door closed, and I realized he'd changed into a Cubs' jersey. A real home game one. A Javier Baez, with the number '9' on the back.

"Damn, you really are a fan."

He smirked, and whipped out a real home game cap, and slipped it on to his head. "It's been a long time since I've been to a game. And we're headed to enemy territory. I need to gird my loins."

Erg, so did I.

Eventually, the pressure went down as we walked toward the subway. I pulled out my phone and checked the trains we needed. I wasn't ashamed in having no idea where Citi Field was earlier in the week. I was a Cubs fan, not a Mets fan. But as it turned out, it was way closer than Yankee Stadium and we just had to change at Grand Central for the 7 Train to Mets-Willets Point.

Easy.

Also, kind of fun. Living in New York was still a bit of a novelty to me, so taking the trains and saying things like 'the 7 train' made me feel like I knew what I was doing.

Getting on the 7 at Grand Central, we were politely, and good naturedly booed as we took our seats. Chase was laughing, and I stood and gave everyone the finger. They booed and laughed louder and I sat down.

"I didn't realize they were *friendly*," Chase hissed.

"Most places you go, the sports teams are a

friendly competition," I answered. "The only place you'll ever feel threatened is by the bleacher creatures, and in Philadelphia. Don't ever go to a game in Philly decked out in the opposing team. They will hound your ass."

He laughed. "Is that experience?"

"Damn straight." I nodded. "Dad took us once and that was a disaster. We bought cheap Phillies T-shirts and changed in the bathrooms."

Chase was laughing, hard. "Seriously?"

"Yeah, but the cheesesteak was worth it."

Shaking his head, we watched the dark tunnels flicker by as the wheel screamed along the metal tracks. The light from the car shone off cables attached to the wall, and we sped under the East River out toward Queens and the baseball game.

I really hoped that this was enough of an apology. Because being near someone as hot and *nice* as Chase was absolutely going to leave me with zipper imprints on my dick.

CHAPTER
NINE

CHASE

MARCUS HAD ABSOLUTELY SHOCKED ME with the tickets. I had no idea he felt that bad about skipping out on the furniture moving party. I would have been less forceful on the whole thing if I knew guilt was going to play into it.

At the same time, the guy was really excited to be going to a game.

Frankly, so was I. I hadn't been in years. I'd gone once or twice when I'd first gotten to the city, seeing if I could pledge my sort-of allegiance to either the Mets or the Yankees. While the Yankees had been fun, cheering against my whole childhood in favor of the Mets had not happened.

Eventually, I just forgot about it. There was no one to enjoy the games with anyway. And going on my own wasn't washing away the hurt.

This, though, in my native ritual dress, with

someone also in their ritual dress, had the potential to be a shit ton of *fun*. I knew we were going to be ribbed and teased, but as long as we weren't in with the bleacher creatures, we'd be just fine.

Jeers and boos followed us off the train, down the walkway, across the lawns and up to the entrance of Citi Field. By the time we were halfway between the stadium and the train, I was proudly waving my middle finger at the other fans along with Marcus.

This was more fun than I'd had in a long time.

Walking into Citi Field, I craned my neck around. This was way, *way* nicer than Shea stadium had been. That thing had been falling down around the team's ears. Marcus flashed the tickets and we headed into the stands. We were half an hour early, so there was a bit of time before everything filled up.

Since he'd bought the tickets, I bought the beers. I knew he'd had a fondness for Brooklyn Brown, so I got two very expensive cups of it, as well as two pretzels. I handed one of each to him.

Leading us on, we walked closer and closer to home base. Down into the front sections right behind the plate and finally, he motioned to two seats just outside of the first base line at home.

I stared at him. "Are you fucking with me?"

"What? I couldn't get them any closer—"

"These are season seats, man, you can't just—"

"I got them off someone who has season passes. They weren't able to make this game and had them up on StubHub at a reduced rate. I figure it was a good deal. Since we aren't cheering for the home team, why pay full price at their home?"

"Boo!" someone screamed from above us.

We both flipped the bird up toward them.

I plunked my ass into the seat next to him. "Marcus. I didn't know you felt this bad about ditching me—"

"You've been more kind about my dog than I had any right to expect. Changing your place around, not complaining, walking him when I couldn't get home. Sit your ass in that seat and help me feel better about how I've taken advantage of you."

I could think of better ways to take advantage of me.

The thought shocked me so much, I almost dropped my beer. Marcus managed to grab my hand at the last second and steady it.

A bolt of lightning went through my fingers at his touch.

I froze. What the shit was that? What was going on? He'd only saved my beer that I'd paid too much for. He'd only brought me to a baseball came to make up for being a bit of a user. He'd only gotten some of the best seats I'd ever been in for a game. He'd only texted me every day, saying hello and chatting about stupid mundanities.

Oh, and I'd only masturbated to his voice three times a week for the past two years.

Jesus, Mary, Joseph, and the camel.

Was I *falling* for Marcus Chastain Romano?

"Got it?"

I looked at him and realized he was staring at my

beer.

"Oh, yeah, yeah. I'm good." I slipped it into the cup holder and promptly shoved a large portion of my pretzel in my mouth.

"So, does this go toward making up for the dog?"

I chewed as fast as I could while I was nodding. "You did not have to do this at all, Marc. Not at all. This is a lot."

"You've been one of four people since I moved here who have gone out of their way to help me. And I'm grateful. When I saw the Cubs shrine, I figured it would be cool to catch a game."

He took a thoughtful bite of the pretzel. "So, what did you say you do for living?"

Polite chat. Right. That was a normal buddy thing to do. I swallowed hard before I answered. I was feeling really, really off balance at that moment. "Graphic design. I usually work on online commercial placements, but they have me taking over my co-worker's billboard next week."

"Is he that bad?"

"No, he had to take FMLA...uh, family medical leave. I don't really get along with him that great. He's an arrogant asshole and a bit of a scatter brained twink, but I think that part is an act."

"Don't hold back now." He laughed, clearly unaware of what my brain was doing in my head at that moment.

I forced my thoughts to circle back to Felix and his weird change of attitude in the past week. "You know, come to think of it, something was very different about him this week. Usually he flames in, shits all over everyone's good day and flounces back out, but this week, he was very quiet and didn't seem to want to be seen. That's not his thing."

Marcus was looking at me strangely. "Are you...homophobic?"

"What?" Everything else in my brain evaporated.

"You're using some pretty harsh language here, man. I mean flaming? Flouncing?"

Now I was confused. "Well, I mean...he's gay and he pisses me off all the time with his over-the-top antics when I know he's not really like that..."

"There's nothing wrong with being gay."

"Of course not—oh shit." I gasped and put a hand over my mouth. "You really think I'm being a homophobe right now, don't you?"

"I'm just expecting you to call him a fa—"

I slapped my hand over his mouth. "Don't say it. Don't. I'm not going to. Felix's ostentatious flouncing and flaming bothers me because it makes everyone in the office think that all gay men act like that. And we don't."

I felt his jaw go slack behind my hand and his eyes grew wide.

My eyes were wide too. "Wait, Marcus. You didn't realize I was gay?"

He shook his head in the negative and I dropped my hand from his mouth. "You are?"

I nodded.

"Oh, my God." He went bright red with embarrassment. "Chase, I'm sorry. I didn't realize...

Holy crap my gaydar is broken."

The laugh just slipped out, catching the attention of some of the people sitting nearby. I clapped a hand over my mouth and manage to calm down. "I didn't realize you didn't realize." I patted his hand. "It's fine. No harm no foul, here. But you can understand why I get mad at Felix?"

He laughed and nodded. "Yeah. I'm a former high school wide receiver and gay as the day is long. Him acting over the top about being gay can make some gay guys uncomfortable."

"I've shared a cube with the guy for three years, and I've seen him act like his true self a few times. I often wonder what he gains from being so flamboyant as an act. I know some men are just naturally twinks, and with them it comes off way more honest, sincere, and natural. Noah and Uriah's younger brother is a sweet, soft, flamboyant man who really just pulls you in with his charms and silly nature. And to see Felix trying so damn hard to be silly, charming, and sincerer by acting like a damn fool...it makes me mad."

Marcus nodded. "I get that. I hate being pigeonholed for being gay." He flopped his hand, making his wrist limp. "I can't tell you how many times I was asked why I wasn't wearing a dress."

"You do not have the legs for it." I deadpanned.

"Girlfriend you have no idea," he answered, rolling his eyes.

We collapsed into gales of laughter and it really felt like a wall had come down between us. I'd been comfortable around him before, but now it felt like...

I cut the thought off. *Enjoy the game, asshole.*

"So, what do you do for work?"

He held up a finger as he finished chewing his bite of pretzel. "I'm a sound engineer, for now. I've been late this week because we kept having to re-engineer these four commercials. Turns out, someone had access to our server and was uploading new cuts without change orders. That's all been sorted and we're starting over on Monday."

I hadn't missed the statement early on in his explanation. "For now?"

He nodded. "I went to Boston Conservatory. I actually want to break into voice acting. Not just commercials, but I'd love to do cartoons and movies. Be the next voice of the Enterprise...uh, what are they on now? G? H?"

Swallowing hard, I pursed my lips. "Actually? The next in the canon is 'S'."

"Oh, no. Are you a Trekkie?"

"Trekk*er.* Not as hardcore. I'm not going to sit here defend *Plato's Children* as a marvelous piece of cinema because it has the first interracial kiss. The story was shit, and there were undertones of forced intercourse."

"That whole little speech was not the speech of someone lightly involved in the fandom." Marcus' eyebrow rose as he considered me.

I coughed. "Well."

"Well what?" He was desperately hiding a laugh.

"I might have been into it a lot more when I was

in high school. And maybe I read the Memory Alpha wiki once in a while to see if I remember anything."

Marcus started laughing, unable to hold it anymore. "It's no worse than me reading Wookiepedia for shits and giggles."

Slumping into my chair, I laughed along with him. "Okay, fine, fair enough. Trekker and a Star Woid." When we finally calmed from laughing, I glanced over. "Really, though? A voice actor?"

I knew exactly what I was doing.

He nodded. "Yeah. Someone told me long ago that while I might not be able to sing well, my voice was clear and strong and I kind of took that to heart. I went to Boston to see if I could develop it. I did pretty well. I have a second income from my audiobooks."

There it was—my opening. "I saw that on the wall of fame in your apartment. I hope you don't mind I was snooping."

"It's on the wall and you've been in my place more than I have lately." The second half of his sentence was bitter, but only just.

"What's it for?"

"Male narrator of the year."

I swatted his arm. "I can read that. What book did you get it for?"

He scratched his head, and blushed. "*Too Far the Near Shore.*"

I gasped, loudly. "Holy shit, that was you? You read a Pulitzer nominated book?"

"Yeah," he said, quietly. "I don't do them under

my real name. You can read, you saw it. But the author listened to some of my other audiobooks and he liked the voice. So he went out of his way to find me and beg me to record it."

"Why aren't you crowing that from the nearest trees? That book was amazing, and the audiobook was...phenomenal. Wait...did you also do the sound engineering on it? All the special effects?"

"I have a second award for that," he answered.

"Oh my *God*, Marcus! Why don't you have your name in lights over the next Disney Animated marquee?"

He swallowed, nervously. "Because just about everything else I've ever narrated has been gay or straight romance." His eyes slipped to mine. "And the world doesn't look kindly on romance at all. It's considered a crap genre, even if it is full of the world's bestselling books at any given time."

I could see him wilting. "What do you mean?"

"I mean, if you tell someone you work with the romance genre, in just about any capacity, they look down their nose at you. That Thomas Renault hunted me down to do the book was a fucking miracle. No one in academia wants to consider the genre as a legitimate pursuit. Despite there being romance all over the literary canon. DuMaurier, the Brontës, Bram Stoker, Shakespeare, Chaucer, Wilde, Hugo, Morrison... Genre literature is not respected. Not horror, not sci-fi, not fantasy, not romance. The academics consider it below them, when in fact it is the very essence of the human condition. Even disguised as the Night King, Maud'dib, or a Langolier."

Staring out at the field, I blinked a few times. "Is your degree in Arts or Psychology? Because, damn, dude."

He sighed. "That escalated quickly."

The laugh burst out of me again. This man was brilliant and funny. No wonder I agreed to walk his dog.

CHAPTER TEN

MARCUS

HE WAS GAY.

Chase was gay.

He was into men. He liked dick.

Oh, dear God in Heaven, he played for my team and I was so, so screwed. It was bad enough I had been staring after his ass when I thought he was straight, but then I had seen his naked torso. Now, all that combined with the fact that he was gay.

Done. Gone. Pure whack-off fantasy for the next two months.

I wanted to weep into my hands. Because for all the interest in him I had shoved back down, he didn't show even the slightest interest in me. That kinda sucked.

Somehow, I managed to keep my head about me, and steered my brain and dick away from the man back to the game.

As it turned out, the Mets beat the tar out of the Cubs. Didn't surprise either of us, and while we were fans, it became clear we were casual fans. Didn't mean the loss didn't hurt. Every Cubs loss hurt, but I'd stopped being achingly disappointed.

The crowd was still booing us cheerfully on the way back to the train, and we didn't care. We just kept handing out the middle fingers and heading for the station.

"Got any plans for dinner?" Chase asked.

"Not really," I answered.

"How about we grab some Thai from Chez Trinh, and we can crash at my place for a few. Since I have a bigger couch and a television."

"A television, how fancy," I mocked.

"Well, it's bigger than yours."

I choked. "You really want to go there?"

He turned bright pink. "Jesus. No. Not even close."

We laughed as another group of fans accosted us good-naturedly on the train.

"You like Thai?" I asked Chase.

"I like anything that you can't find in Buttfuck Nowhere. Thai, Ethiopian, Indian, Afghani, Filipino, sushi, Korean. Whatever. Anything not Chinese and burgers. I like burgers, but not as a habit."

"I'm going to wager that you're from a small town and couldn't wait to get out."

"Half right," Chase said, quietly. "I am from a small town, but *they* couldn't wait to get me out."

I felt a little crestfallen on that. "I'm sorry. I didn't

mean to bring up anything bad."

He waved me off. "Long time ago. I'm happy and well established here with a great group of friends."

"Except Felix."

Chuckling, he nodded. "Except Felix."

The Thai place was between our subway stop and our apartment building. We probably ordered enough for an army between the two of us, but it wouldn't go to waste.

Chase led us up to the door, and then pointed to mine. "Get the pooch. Bring him over and we'll take him out for a walk later."

"Good call," I said. "There's also a really good cupcake place on the other side of the square. We'll get dessert."

Pollux happily trotted over to the other door as soon as I opened mine and wandered right in. I stared at him and followed after locking mine.

"My dog is a traitor."

Chase laughed from where he was in the kitchen. "Have a seat. I'm sure your dog is already on the couch."

I turned around and found the dog in the living room, on the couch. "Pollux, you can be a real jerk sometimes," I said, sitting down next to him.

"Turn on the TV. Put whatever you like on. I'll be there in a second. Beer?"

"God, no...no more beer. Soda? Water? Anything like that is fine." I grabbed the remote and clicked on the television.

He had a super extra smart TV that he could

apparently listen or watch just about anything on. I saw the Audible app and clicked on it for the hell of it.

The first seven titles were mine.

Not my lit fic ones, either. All seven were my gay romance reads.

Holy crap.

I tossed a look over my shoulder back at the kitchen, and saw he was still puttering around. I click on the first title and...there were bookmarks. About ten of them. I navigated to the first one, and checked the volume before hitting play.

I *hated* listening to my voice, but there it was quietly rising out of the speakers at one of the dirtiest parts of the book I had narrated. I skipped to the next. Same thing—filth. They were all marking the dirty parts of the books.

"What are you doing?"

I slammed on the power button and whirled up and off the couch. Chase was standing in the door holding plates and the Thai food. "Uh..."

He slumped a bit, and dropped the food on the coffee table. "Here. Enjoy. I'll get the drinks." He turned to walk back to the kitchen.

"Chase."

He stopped. I took a deep breath.

"I'm sorry. I saw my name and you were so excited about my lit fic book, I thought..." I took a deep breath. "I was curious what you were bookmarking in the other titles."

Shaking his head, he kept walking.

Shit, fuck, *damn.*

I stood in the middle of his living room, looking around like an idiot, trying to figure out what to do. As soon as I heard the first bit of dirty dialogue, I should have just quit the app and went to the regular programing. Pollux whined from where he was on the couch.

The first thing I should've done after that humiliating move was just grabbed my dog and left.

I didn't.

He walked back in, and sighed sitting down.

"I'm sorry," I said. "That was wrong. That was an invasion of your privacy and I'm sorry."

He pursed his lips. "It's really not all that different than me going through your pictures when you're not there."

"I don't want this to be awkward."

He tossed his head back. "Oh that ship sailed when I realized you're Marcus Chastain, award winning audiobook narrator."

"Wait, when did you realize that?" I was genuinely confused.

"The first night I walked Pollux."

"I thought you only knew *Too Far*?"

Chase rolled his head to the cushion on the back of the couch and laughed. "I bought that because I bought all the other ones."

Oh, *shit*. I plunked my ass back on the couch. "So this has been slightly awkward for you all along. I'm just boarding the awkward boat now."

He let out a breath. "Yeah. I guess we could say that."

"So, uh...you like gay romance, eh?"

The laugh he let out peeled through the room, startling my dog—and me, to be honest.

"That would also be an understatement." He sat up and grabbed the remote, turning on some streaming music so the room had a softer feel to it. Much better than just seconds before.

"Why so many of mine?"

His eyebrow arched up delicately and he cocked his head. "Your voice, man. You have a *fuck me* bedroom voice. It makes..." He hung his head. "Jesus. I have to explain this, don't I?"

"You don't. I can go."

His hand landed on my knee, and he looked slightly panicked. "No, I can explain. But it's a bit of TMI, when it's all said and done."

I leaned back against the couch cushions. "I'm pretty hard to shock. Hit me."

"I masturbate to them."

I was pretty sure my eyebrows flew off my face, and my dick hit the back of my zipper with an audible *ting*. "Okay, you got me."

Chase was bright, bright red, and he had moved his hand from my knee, and was nervously lacing and unlacing his fingers. "I'm a demi."

"A what?"

"Demi. Romantic." He strung the two words together. "I don't feel sexual desire until after I've formed an emotional and intellectual bond. But that doesn't mean I don't get horny. The problem lies in the fact that regular porn does *plllbbbttt* shit for me. Normal male visual and sensory stimulation don't work for getting me there. I need more. I need a formed attachment.

"At first, I would read the M-M romances a few times and feel like I got to know the characters. That helped. But when I found audiobooks... It was a whole new world. And listening to your sultry tones added another layer to it. So I listened. Over and over. And I have the stories memorized."

"And you..." God, who was I discussing this like a mature adult? I hadn't once used the term *pull your pud* in relation to his dick and my voice. "...would use that."

Chase nodded once. "I need to know people before I can feel sexual desire, and reading and listening to the entire *Toxic Kiss* series in your voice..."

He let out a breath and rolled his eyes. "Shit. This is why I don't date. This is why every single relationship I have ever had has failed. It's so fucking hard to explain this. Kieran was good with it, but there was no spark—and other men I've gone out with don't get it. For them, sex is mechanical, a necessary, enjoyable biological development." He tapped his forehead. "I get stuck being the town faggot who doesn't like to just have sex for shits and giggles and get run off because the mayor's son wanted a convenient ass to play with."

"And you weren't playing."

Chase turned and stared at me. "He was my literal nemesis for all my life. A bully and a jerk. And then he discovers he's gay and I'm going to bend over and let him fuck me? Hell. No."

Snatching a carton of Pad See Ew, he stabbed his

chopsticks into it angrily and shoveled some into his mouth.

I couldn't hold back the smirk on my lips. "So...you like gay romance, then."

He choked on the noodles and stared at me. Half a second later, all the tension in the air broke and we both burst into laughter. I had to grab the carton of food from him before he dumped it on the couch, and we just took a minute to let ourselves laugh and collect our thoughts.

Holding up a finger, he shook it in my face. "I just want you to know that I don't *only* read and listen to gay romance. I also read lit fic, straight romance, urban fantasy, and paranormal romance."

I giggled like a toddler. "I'll bet you read all the straight stuff just to hear about the male main character's junk and prowess."

He looked offended. "I'm sorry, there's another reason?"

"Well, it's okay if you're a little homoflexible."

Chase shivered dramatically. "Ugh. Vagina." He drooped a bit, and sighed. "That makes me sound like Felix. I don't have a problem with women."

"I didn't think you did," I answered. "How old?"

"Well, I think I suspected when I was really young, like seven, or eight. But I didn't know how to articulate that. When I kissed Vicky Turnbull at the eighth grade dance, I knew for sure I didn't like girls because I wished she was Brad Vandergraff." He sighed heavily. "Brad..."

I laughed. "Brad, eh?"

"I tutored him. He was just the worst at anything

literary or artsy. He couldn't string a sentence together if you gave him the string and laid out the words in order. Math whiz. Tutored me so I didn't fail miserably."

"What happened to dreamy Brad Vandergraff?"

"He kissed Vicky." His voice was *so* put out at that. It was adorable.

Oh shit.

He picked up the carton of Thai noodles again. "You?"

"I was pretty sure I was straight, I didn't even mind kissing girls. Irene, Marcia... I even scandalized Najwa's family by kissing her. Thankfully, her parents were trying to be more open than strict traditional Iraqi, so it turned out fine."

He watched me, and shoveled more food into his mouth. "How'd you finally realize?" The words came out around the food, and I didn't know how he did that. But I wanted to see him try with my cock in there.

Oh *shit*.

"I...uh. I dated Emma for two years, so when we were seventeen, it just seemed the right time to take the next step in our relationship."

"Didn't work out?"

"I had to pretend she was Johnny Depp to finally seal the deal."

"Pirate Johnny, Edward Scissorhands Johnny?"

I coughed. "Ed Wood Johnny."

"Oh, you are *so gay*!"

Sighing, I picked up my carton for Lad Na. "I am. I really am. I think it's why I take on all the gay romance novels that I do. They make me feel like the world may finally someday just *get over itself* and let men love men or women or men and women."

He gasped, "Ménages?"

"Better." I leaned in close. "Harems. Why choose?"

"Oh to have a harem at my disposal." He sighed.

"You know there's a whole subgenre of reverse harems, right?"

"You can't have a *reverse* harem. A stable of available sex is still a stable of available sex." The slow rise of his eyebrow was goddamned adorable.

"It's a way to connotate that there are stallions in the stables, not fillies," I explained. "And some of them? Are really hot when the men get to ride each other while the others watch, or ride along."

"Are we comparing human sexual interaction to horses right now?" Chase looked confused and distressed.

"Wanna read one? I'm supposed to record the audio for it next week."

"Oh, sweet Jesus, no."

"The two guys didn't know they were bi before getting together with the heroine." I waggled my eyebrows. "Lots of dirty details."

"And straight sex."

"Not just. Just yes...mixed in."

"Fine, I'll take a copy."

I started laughing. "You're easy to please."

Chase grabbed the remote, and flicked on the streaming options for television. "I'm not. I'm really, really not."

CHAPTER ELEVEN

CHASE

MARCUS WOUND UP ON MY COUCH on Monday night, and we ate pizza. We talked for hours about stupid shit like my coworkers and the graphic design world.

Pollux barked at the wall all night.

Tuesday was Indian. Hours and hours about how bad the last *Superman* movie was despite the absolute gorgeous nature of Henry Cavill.

Pollux was still barking at the wall.

Wednesday was German. I had no idea there was a take out German place nearby, but the brats were to die for, and no one had ever turned down kartofflepuffers. We picked up on a bad superheroes movies in the 90s and lamented the loss of good quality bad movies like *Meteor Man.* I also missed campy *Batman,* but only a little.

Pollux, still on a mission to make the wall his

bitch, barked all night long.

Thursday night, he brought Mexican from the little place near his office that he hadn't been able to get off his mind for two weeks. We talked about the stupidity it took to allow some random person access to the internal files of a business.

"I mean, it's all solved now, and poor Hardy feels just effing awful," he said, gesturing with a burrito. "Jerry just cannot find someone who can help him catch up on years, and I mean *years* of backlog on updates and organization. I don't know why Hardy didn't say something."

"Saying something is a hallmark of our generation," I said. "We were never brushed off when we asked for help. Older generations were taught to suffer through." I pulled my empanada in two pieces to let it cool a bit more. "My grandfather used to refuse to take his Ultram because he swore the doctor had told him it was better to suffer through the pain. Meanwhile, you and I both know suffering through is utter shit medical advice. Medicine exists to help us get through things like pain and help us breathe."

"Which is why we ask for help. We don't have to be these masculine macho badasses anymore."

I huffed. "Speak for yourself. I'm a masculine macho badass every day."

"Uh..."

"Oh fuck off, I look good in lavender."

"You do." He nodded.

Huh... Moving on...

"If you know anyone who is looking for an IT

position with good benefits and a nice boss who won't fire their ass for a major fuck up, send them my way. Hardy is close to breaking." Marcus shrugged.

I sat up from the cushions. "Actually, I might. He's trying to get his life back together after some shit, and I think that he might be perfect. He needs to not be around people much, but he's amazing at IT."

"Do it! Give him my number and get me his resume!" Marcus fist pumped, and laughed. "Hardy will be so grateful for any kind of help. No one realized how overwhelmed the poor guy was."

I smiled. "Raph is a good guy, and his brothers are worried about him. If we can get him back into the—"

"Ssh!" Marcus snapped, putting a finger to my lips.

Lightning shot through me from the tip of his finger through my entire body.

His eyes snapped to mine.

He felt it too.

"...*mrow*..."

Pollux jumped up on the couch and started barking at the wall.

"Pollux, hush!" I said, and pushed him down off the couch.

"...mrow..."

Marcus and I stared at each other.

"Is that a cat?" I breathed.

"I think it's a kitten." His voice was hushed.

"...mrow..."

"Oh, my God," I whispered. "There are kittens in the wall."

He leapt up from the couch and ran out the door of my apartment. I heard him banging next door for a moment and then he was back.

With a toolbox.

"What—"

"We have to get them out," he said, breathlessly. "We don't know if the mama can get to them, and we sure as Hell don't know if they can get out."

He put the tools on the coffee table as I scrambled to get the food into the kitchen—so we wouldn't mess it up, and Pollux wouldn't help himself to a burrito.

I came back in to find him gently tapping on the wall. As he got close to one spot near the end, the plaintive meows grew a little louder. He moved away again, and they grew soft. He checked up and down and finally settled on a spot.

"Here. Hand me the grease pencil."

Plucking it out of the top tray, he took it from me and started making a square. "I'm going to start above them, and see if we can't lift them out."

He dropped the pencil back in and grabbed a yellow box with lights on it, and pressed the two buttons on the side. It beeped and I realized it was a stud finder. He placed it on the wall and found the beams that were on either side of the meowing.

Handing it back to me, he pointed to the box. "Chisel. The thinner one. And a hammer."

I grabbed the clear yellow handle and presented it to him. He held his hand out for the small ball-peen hammer I was offering and tapped the handle. The chisel plowed through the wallboard, and he made a quick, neat line across the wall. He went up about six inches and made another.

The cries from behind the wallboard were desperate and frightened and I couldn't believe we were digging a hole in the wall to save kittens.

A quick line of cracks down the center of the wallboard square, and Marcus was able to pop the first piece off in one shot, and then pop the other off.

"Flashlight?"

There was a pen light in the top tray so that's what I handed him. He pointed it down and I heard scrabbling against the wall.

"Oh, my *God*, they are so cute!" he declared. "Looks like...four of them. I think I can just reach in and grab them."

"Wait, let's get something to put them in," I said, and raced for the bedroom. I found my tall laundry basket and inverted it, leaving dirty socks and underwear all over the floor. Didn't care at that moment. I grabbed a fresh towel from the bathroom and tucked it at the bottom.

Marcus was still peering into the hole, and making soft sounds at the creatures. His eyes were shining with delight as I put the laundry basket next to him.

His hand reached in and he grabbed the first of the litter: a tiny, wide-eyed, big-eared calico ball of fluff.

"Well, hello, pretty thing!" He lowered her into the basket, and fished out the other three: an all-black sleek, thin boy, a black and white tuxedo girl, and a creamy tabby boy. They were all situated at the bottom, looking a little dirty, but no obvious fleas and no issues that we could see.

"Where's the mom?" I asked, peering in.

"We're going to have to lure her out with the kittens and food."

"I don't have cat food."

"Tuna?"

"That I have," I answered. "But these guys need milk and a bath."

He nodded. "That they do."

Which was how I wound up running down Thompson Street for the Pet Bar at a quarter to eight, hoping they would be open until I dragged my ass through the doors.

MOTHER CAT had been more than willing to hop out of the wall for tuna and her babies. By the time I had gotten back with flea meds, Dawn soap, Kitten Replacement Milk, bottles, nipples, wet and dry food, and a cat carrier, Marcus had coaxed her out and she was in with her kittens in the basket.

We'd washed each of them, including Mother Cat—which was not fun, but easier when we had the kittens on the counter with her, and settled them all back in the basket, letting MC feed them.

"You're a daddy." Marcus chuckled.

"I can't keep them!"

"Please," he said.

"Dude, I cannot keep five cats!"

"You could keep Mother," he suggested. "The

kittens will be easy to place."

I swallowed. "They need to go to the vet, tomorrow."

He agreed, "They do. We've done as much as we can, but the vet needs to check them out. Can you handle that tomorrow?"

"I mean, I guess so. I haven't taken a day off from work in months." I stared down into the basket at the five of them. MC was a beautiful animal, white with gray and orange tabby spots, and young I guessed. The cream tabby boy was also—

I groaned, "God, I cannot have a cat!"

"You've already picked them out, haven't you?"

"Shit. Yes."

He patted me on the shoulder. "Ever had cats before?"

"Yes," I groaned. "I grew up on a farm-ish thing."

"Farm-ish thing?" His eyes danced with humor.

"It's midnight. I'm exhausted. I cannot brain to make the words go for now. I need to sleep."

He grew serious. "You'll be okay over here with Mama and her kittens?"

"Perfectly fine." I sighed.

"Okay, I'm going to take Pollux out for a quick walk and head to bed. Call me and let me know how it goes tomorrow with the kitties?"

"I'll even send pictures."

"Good man." He nodded. "Kitty pictures are always welcome."

"Won't you make Pollux jealous?"

Marcus blinked a few times and looked over at his

dog, sleeping near the door. "Uh, he barks at walls."

Our eyes went wide, and turned slowly to look at the dog. Marcus looked back at me, and gasped, "He heard the kittens. The whole time. They're about five weeks old..."

"They wouldn't have started meowing with any kind of vocal range until now," I continued, "but we don't have dog ears. He would have heard them scraping around and meowing for mama all along."

Both of us dropped down to the dog and started giving him pats, pets, and belly rubs. We were cooing over the same dumb mutt who barked me into another room. But he had probably saved the kittens because we had no idea how they got in and out. Which was something else I had to talk to the landlord about.

Pollux looked both pleased and annoyed with us, and as a show of gratitude stood up sleepily, tripped over his own ungainly feet, and slammed me into Marcus, sending us sprawling on the floor.

Or, more correctly, sending Marcus to the floor on his back and taking away my support, and send me sprawling across Marcus.

Across his broad shoulders. His narrow waist. His firm six pack. His sculpted pecs. His defined thighs.

Fuuuuck.

His eyes were an amber brown, ringed in a dark soil color, and his pupils were huge. His hair was a dirty, light brown, almost blond and now a mess from flopping over. He was shocked, surprised, unsure, and *really turned on.*

A flood of emotions poured through me, wrecking me, eroding walls and dams and levees that normally blocked and redirected all this shit. This time, it plowed right through me.

Marcus Romano was fucking gorgeous.

And I wanted to get to know him even more.

Before I could put any thoughts in my head, or pull any out or screw all this up by thinking, I pressed forward and slammed my mouth over his.

He let out a little gasp, just a little one, and then *took the fuck over*.

His tongue pressed against me, pushed against my lips and invaded my mouth. As demanding as that was, his lips were liquid, warm, inviting on mine. He moved them slowle and carefully, as his tongue did the same with mine. I felt pure heat race through me, and the languid desire seemed to follow, landing in my balls.

I hadn't felt this hard in years.

While his assault on my mouth continued, his fingers laced up into my hair, scraping my scalpe lightly, teasing the nape of my neck. His other hand slipped down my back, tracing my spine, and spreading wide over the globe of my ass.

He squeezed, slowly.

The sensation of his heightening pressure on me through my jeans did crazy things to my brain, my whole body.

I felt like I was going to come in my pants like I was thirteen again.

With a quick move, Marcus rolled us so he was

above me and his weight on me felt so damn amazing. I could feel his hard cock pressing against mine through the sweat pants we were wearing.

"Holy God, Chase..." His breath was ragged as he leaned his forehead on mine.

"You kiss like a dream."

He moved his hips over mine, rubbing us together. "I want to drag you into that bed. But if I do that we'll never climb out tomorrow."

I reached down between us and slipped my hand under the waistband of his pants. "You're absolutely correct on that." I trailed my fingers down his erection and cupped his balls. "But we're not getting up until you get off."

His hand didn't bother trying to be subtle. He shoved the pants off my hips, dragging my boxers with them, and let them rest halfway down my thighs. I took his cue and did the same with his.

Marcus' big hand brought our cocks together, and he held them tightly, slipping his thumb over the head and gathering the pre-cum, moving his hand up and down. "I need to make you come, Chase."

"Yes, God, yes," I hissed.

He leaned down to my ear, and for the first time in the weeks we'd spent together, I heard Marcus Chastain's delicious *fuck me* bedroom voice. "I have wanted to touch you almost since the day I met you. I have craved your taste like a man in a desert craves water."

Oh, God. All I could do was whimper at his words. So many times I heard those perfect tones in my ears when I listened to him narrate those filthy words, his sounds, his breaths in the headphones, while my hand made quick work of my own cock.

Now, they were *his* words, and his hand, and he was above me pressing me to the floor of my own bedroom. Real, live, sexual, sultry, and *oh so fucking good*.

I hadn't even realized I was building the emotional connection I needed with him for this to happen, and it felt better than just about anything else—or one—I had ever done in my life.

"You feel like steel in my hand, Chase. Your skin is hot and you're so perfectly thick against me."

"Marcus..."

"I want your cum on me."

There was no stopping me at that point. I arched into his body, pressing our dicks against his stomach and the orgasm just roared out of my body, spilling every last drop of cum I had in my balls all over him, me, our cocks, his hand, our shirts. Not even three strokes of his massive hand later, he roared his climax as well, joining his release with mine all over our bodies.

He released our spent erections a moment after, and he wrapped his hands under my arms, rolling us to our sides.

I was staring into his amazing eyes.

"Hi."

The blast of air escaped me unbidden. "Fuck."

Marcus laughed. "Good?"

"Sweet Jesus, yes."

He leaned in and kissed me, a lazy languid motion of his lips over mine. "I really wish I didn't have to go to work tomorrow."

"You really wanted me all this time?" I asked.

"Even when I thought you were straight. You have a very hot ass, Mister Garcia."

I looked down between us. "We should clean up."

He closed his eyes and pinched his nose. "I am going to go back to my apartment and clean up. If I clean up here, we're just going to end up naked in bed."

"You make that sound so bad."

Marcus smirked. "It's not bad. But it's Thursday and you need time to absorb all this." He pressed his forehead to mine. "I did some reading on demisexuality, and you need to process everything that's happened. I don't want to scare you, or scare you off."

"Well, that's very considerate of you, Mister Romano." I grinned. "Wikipedia?"

"Nope, found all kinds of other resources." He was very proud of himself. "You have to take the kittens to the vet tomorrow, and I have an important client meeting. It's smarter if I sleep in my own place."

I nodded. "It makes a lot of sense." I kissed his nose. "Dinner? Tomorrow night?"

He gave me a blinding, full tooth grin. "It's a date."

God, it *was* a date.

CHAPTER TWELVE

MARCUS

CHASER: *GOOD MORNING*, VOCE.

> **Chaser**: *I hope your day is as amazing as my night was.*
> **Marcus302**: *Ooh, did you have a good time?*
> **Chaser**: *Why yes I did. In fact I have the hottest, frottiest rug burn on my ass ever.*
> **Marcus302**: *I forgot about the berber!*
> **Chaser**: *Why do you think this is a problem? I'm going to think about you and that lovely dick every time I move in a chair today.*

Mrph. Now I was going to think about rug burn on his ass, all day.

"I really hope you're looking at your phone," Hardy mumbled. "No one should smile at their crotch like that."

Jerry laughed. "Well, he does like—"

"Jerry!" Sorcha snapped, trying not to laugh.

"Yeah, my own doesn't usually bring me that much joy," I answered, sleeping the phone. "I was however talking to one that does."

Sorcha groaned, but the tension in the room from the meeting we were waiting on broke and everyone chuckled. Much better than just a few minutes before.

We were going over the new contract for a ten-episode series on a streaming network that the network and the producers were sure would get renewed. This was big stuff and the whole reason I hadn't I picked Chase up off the floor and shagged his ass raw last night.

This was important. I needed my name on productions, on big successful ones. It wasn't using my voice, but between the audiobooks and this production, it was the right combination for my resume.

The speaker in the middle of the table beeped, and Vi's voice floated out of the speaker. "Jerry, the production team is here."

"I'll be right out." He took a deep breath. "I've done a thousand of these, and I still get nervous." Pulling the door open, he headed out and into the lobby.

"You all ready?" Hardy asked, and looked at his new assistant.

Raphael swallowed hard. "Deep end of the pool," he said, nodding.

"If he starts singing *Shallow*, I'm out," Gabe said, but the smile on his face didn't match his anger.

"I can't sing like Gaga," Raph answered.

I patted him on the shoulder. The poor guy was in here for the second day on the job. He was nervous as Hell, but Hardy had liked him so much he'd hired him on the spot. HR was still trying to get everything processed for him, but Jerry was as enthusiastic as Hardy.

We could all see Jerry walking through the hall through the opaque film of the windows, and heard him chatting with the four people following him.

He opened the door and motioned everyone in as we all walked behind our own chairs and pulled them out to sit. With my ass halfway down to the seat, my worst nightmare walked into the room.

Edward George Roberts.

Eddie.

Ed.

The man who had helped to destroy my entire life so badly the implications were still ringing through the past six years.

His eyes landed on me, at first growing round with shock, and then sliding into his snake oil smile I knew too well.

I couldn't be on this contract. I couldn't. It was bad enough I had to do work for him early on, but he didn't know it was me-me then. Now he was staring at me.

"Gentleman, ladies, let's sit and start a conversation about your contract on postproduction sound for this show," an older man with J. Jonah Jameson hair said.

"Sir, if I may," Ed said, leaning forward. "I don't know if we want this particular team."

"Ed, this is the team that did your last episodes of—"

"Hadn't realized that Marcus Romano was part of that," he bit out. "I would have turned down the replacements. Mister Romano doesn't have the best reputation in mixed company."

I slammed my hands on the table and stood. "I'm out. Don't worry about me touching any of your audio. Sorry, Jerry, I'll go work on my other assignments." I snatched my cup of coffee and marched out of the room.

"That solved itself." I heard Ed laugh as the door was closing behind me.

Furious, I marched through the office and back down the stairs to my dungeon studio and slammed the door. I started up all the equipment and ripped the newest paperwork off the wall so I could see what my day was going to look like.

"Marcus!"

I snapped my eyes up to the door. Sorcha was standing there.

"What the fuck is this?"

"I'm off the project," I said. "Don't ask me to go back, don't ask me what this is about. Keep me away from Ed Roberts, and keep him away from me."

"Marc, this is a huge contract. Jerry wants you—"

"Jerry is not the issue. Ed is the issue. He will destroy this, us, the company if I am near him. I need to stay very very far away from him. I should probably take a vacation day every time he comes into the office."

"Jesus, Marc..."

"Go back to the meeting, Sorcha. I'll handle everything else you guys can't during the show."

She hovered in the door and clearly wanted to say something. I held up my hand and turned back to the soundboard. "Just go. Trust me, just go."

She pulled the door closed after a moment and I stared at the lights, knobs, and sliders in front of me.

This sucked.

I stared at the board. I just stared at it. I couldn't think, I couldn't move, I couldn't function. When Sorcha had mentioned Ed, I had hoped it was a one off. Now...I'd been in the same room with him—and I still had a restraining order out against him. I wasn't even supposed to be legally in the same building.

Thumping my head on the board, I stared at the rug. I would have literally been better off with anyone else except Ed. I could handle even the worst of the gang as long as it wasn't Ed.

But it was. And now I had to figure out what the hell to do because I didn't want to lose my job, but I didn't want to invite him into my life, and into the parameters of the restraining order.

Not that there was anything I could do now to stop him. He'd found me, and I was sure he was the same amazing douche he'd been in college.

There was a hand on my shoulder and I looked up. It was Jerry with his tie was undone and he looked frazzled.

"You okay, Marcus?"

"What are you doing? Why aren't you in the conference room—"

"It's all done, Marc. It's two in the afternoon."

I had *lost* five hours of my life. All because of that son of a bitch. He'd managed to black me out again. I struggled to push to my feet. "Jerry, man, I'm sorry. I didn't mean to do that..."

He waved his hand to cut me off. "What happened?"

"I..."

He closed the door. "First. What happened just now? Why are you so disoriented?"

"Blacked out apparently," I said. "Not the first time."

"Drinking? Medical issue?"

"Does bullying count?"

"Yeah, it sure does," Jerry said. "Ed Roberts?"

"Can I not talk about it?"

He shook his head slowly. "No. Because you're on the team, and I want to know what the obstacles are we're up against."

I sat up a little straighter in the chair. "I'm what?"

"You're on the team," he said. "It was non-negotiable. I told them to walk if they thought I was taking you off."

"You..."

"You're part of the team, you're on the team." He nodded. "Now, what's going on, and do I need to know to call 911, or is there something I can do without that?"

I pursed my lips and chewed on my cheek. "I

literally cannot legally be in the room with Ed Roberts. There's a restraining order involved. He and I had...some run ins during college and I just felt better with a legal shield against him."

"Dude, I had no idea. I would never—"

Holding up my hand, I stopped him. "I moved here to get away from the last of the fallout. The last of the fallout was in Troy. I moved back to Troy to get away from the fucking mess that consumed me at Boston Conservatory. It's been five years since I barely made it out alive with a degree. There is absolutely *no way* you could have known that Ed Roberts was my mortal enemy."

His eyebrow rose. "Mortal enemy."

I huffed out a breath. "Yes. Mortal enemy. He fucked me over *so hard* in college." I gasped, "Oh, shit, Chase."

I yanked my phone off the soundboard and swiped it open.

Seventeen messages.

Chaser: On our way! MC is a good kitty.
Chaser: MC doesn't seem to like dogs that are not Pollux.
Chaser: We're in the room!
Chaser: I hope your meeting is going well.
Chaser: Ooh, MC doesn't like the vet!
Chaser: Marcus, can you call me?
Chaser: Please call me as soon as you can.
Chaser: Marcus, I don't want to make these decisions on my own.

Chaser: *MC has cancer. Please call me.*
Chaser: *The vet thinks we can treat it.*
Chaser: *Oh, my god the cost.*
Chaser: *He wants to run more tests on her. I need you to call me, Marc. Please.*
Chaser: *He wants to know if we're going to leave the kittens with her or take them home. I need help with kittens!*
Chaser: *Marcus?*
Chaser: *I'm taking the kittens home. We have the KMR. MC is going to stay for more tests.*
Chaser: *I can't make the decision to put her down.*
Chaser: *Marcus, please...*

Oh, God, I'd fucked that up big time. I always fucked up when it came to Ed Roberts.

Marcus302: *I'm so sorry, Chase. I got stuck in a meeting. Don't put MC down. I'll help with the kittens. We'll figure out what to do.*

I rubbed a hand over my eyes, and Jerry was still staring at me.

"Okay?"

"We rescued cats out of the wall last night, and the mother cat apparently has cancer. I was supposed to be returning the live updates. I hope Chase doesn't hate me for that."

"You clearly had a rough day" he nodded. "So, you're still on my team, and I don't give a rats ass what

Ed Roberts thinks. You missed the fun part where he tried to get his people to walk, and his boss just shot his ass out of the sky with a close-range missile. *'You liked his work a week ago, Ed. Now you find out he's someone you don't like personally and you want to walk? We're signing you up for professional courtesy classes. Sit your ass down.'* It really was glorious, because I'd gotten the 'shithead' vibe from him as soon as he opened his mouth."

"Well, I appreciate that—"

"And," he said, slicing into my words, "now that I know you've got legal issues with Ed Roberts, we are going to put a rider on the contract that requires him to inform us if he is coming on premises so we can arrange to have you elsewhere, even if I have to send you down to Katz's for a fucking sandwich."

He stood. "I hope you like corned beef."

"You don't have to do that—"

"I do, because you are one of the best investments I've made in years. Shut up, take the compliment and check on your boyfriend and the cats."

"He's not my boyfriend."

Jerry stopped in the door. "Friends don't make you smile at your crotch in meetings."

I KNOCKED on the door. "Chase?"

He whipped the door open, and his eyes were bright red. He'd clearly been crying. He had a small black kitten stuck to his shirt and a creamy beige one sitting on his shoulder.

Chase looked fucking adorable.

"I am so sorry," I managed.

Huffing angrily, he walked back into the kitchen to the left, and I guessed I was supposed to follow him.

I clicked the door closed and found him mixing up more KMR for the furballs. Pollux was licking one of the others that was inside a box on the floor.

He finally whirled around, holding the kittens to him and railed at me. "What the hell happened? You couldn't even sneak out to send me a quick message? I could not handle being told this stupid cat we pulled out of a wall last night was dying of cancer and I had to make decisions—"

I took his face in my hands and kissed him, hard. He tasted just as amazing as I remembered from the night before and it took only a moment for him to go from angry to pliant and slip his tongue along mine.

"I'm sorry," I whispered over his lips. "I am. Shit went down at work, and I never meant to ignore you."

He took a deep breath. "I'm sorry. I was freaking out at the cancer diagnosis."

My lips quirked in a smile. "It's going to be fine. I promise. We might not be able to treat her, but we'll make her comfortable, okay?"

He nodded. "Okay. Do you think we should bring her home and let her nurse the kittens?"

"If she's able to, yes, absolutely."

Chase slumped against the counter, picking up a third kitten and dropping her on his shoulder. "I just felt so bad that Mother Cat was so sick. She's so sweet, Marcus. I'm going to keep her if I can."

"Good," I answered. "If we can't get her cured, she'll have a lovely few months or years with you." I picked up the creamy tabby from his arms. "We need to feed these fuzz buckets?"

"Yes, they're all hungry," he said. "The vet said the KMR is good, but they can have a slurry to start weaning them. I can't keep all of them...so I need to find homes for three of them."

He looked at me and sighed. "I'm sorry if I freaked you out. We only had barn cats growing up. If the kittens didn't make it, they didn't make it. We weren't allowed to bring the cats in. Cats were for..."

"I get it," I said.

"I hope I didn't get you in trouble at work?"

"Nah, not at all. That was the asshole rolling up from my nightmares."

Chase handed me a bottle and a cat, and motioned to the table, for me to sit. "Nightmares?" He grabbed two more bottles and sat at the table with me. Putting the kittens on the table, he quickly moved the bottles to where they could grab on to the nipples. "What nightmares?"

"I...kinda don't want to talk about it?" I cocked my head. "It took up too much of my headspace today and I'm done with it. The situation has been handled and it should be fine."

He nodded, but I could tell he wanted to know more. I had literally lost five hours to that shit and didn't want to tell him the whole story. "Can we suffice to say that it happened in college and that's why I'm not further in my career? And the cause of it all walked into my office this morning."

"Okay, yes, I don't mean to pry. We've just been getting to know each other so well and this is the first time we've hit a wall."

I nodded and flipped my kitten over to rub his full tummy while he kept on drinking. "I know. Just give me time."

Chase nodded.

"So. Tell me about MC?"

CHAPTER THIRTEEN

CHASE

I HAD CRIED ALL THE WAY BACK to the apartment after deciding not to make a decision on MC. I wanted someone, anyone, there with me to make the decision.

My worst crime, to my father, was my soft spot. No good red-blooded American male should get upset over a dumb animal. Not even their own dog.

And never ever ask what happened to the animals behind the barn.

But here were these tiny little kittens and their kitty mama, handed a shit start to life and MC wound up with cancer. I immediately asked for the price on her care, to get her in remission or cured.

However, the vet explained that was a worst-case scenario and there were many other possibilities. I trusted her care to him, and took the kittens home. They crawled all over me, looking for their mom, crying until I finally got the KMR mixed up.

"How much do they know about her condition?" Marcus asked.

"Just that there's a mass by her spleen and her white blood count was through the roof," I answered. "If you go with me tomorrow, we can figure out what I need to do."

"What we need to do," he corrected. "I'm partly responsible for these guys. My dingbat dog found them, and we pulled them out of your wall together. If we pool our resources, we might be able to get a little bit further."

"You don't—"

Holding up his hand, he stopped me. "I want to help, Chase. They're adorable and if MC is going to get a good home with you, then I'm happy to help." He tickled the kitten on his lap until she hiccupped and burped.

Marcus was seriously hot. It had freaked me out a bit the night before when I realized we'd somehow forged the connection I needed to start having feelings for him. It had been utterly effortless with him, and that he hadn't realized we were doing it either was adorable.

Once he'd left the night before, I realized he was right—I had needed time to process what I was feeling for him. It hadn't been out of the blue, but that we allowed it to go that far all of a sudden was blowing my mind.

The only thing I was used to feeling was horny with no real desire toward anyone person. Suddenly wanting Marcus overwhelmed me, but at the same time it was right. It was the first time in a long time that I'd felt a spark.

More than a spark.

Marcus was a good man, he was smart, and he was damn good-looking. I wanted to know more. I wanted a repeat of the carpet sex from last night.

"We need to fix the hole in the wall," I said, having no idea why my brain decided on that.

"I know." He nodded. "I'll get the stuff from the hardware store tomorrow, either before or after the vet visit, and we'll have it patched up quick."

I looked at the two kittens now wrestling on the table, and glanced at the one that Pollux had decided he was going to watch over in the box. "Are we still on for dinner?"

"If you feel up to it."

I peered at him. "I feel more than up to it."

His smirk was delightful. He stood and put the little half asleep ball of fuzz in the box with her brother. "How about if we order in, and see what comes up."

Smirking back, I canted my head and stared him dead in the eye. "I know what's going to come up. It's going to be my cock. And I hope you have plans for that."

"Yes, duh?" He laughed. "Okay, then. I think maybe we *should* go out and get food. Because I have feeling that if we stay in, your sheets are going to be a sticky mess."

"I certainly hope so." Oh, I forgot that sex-driven

me had absolutely no filter.

Marcus didn't seem to be offended by that. He tossed his head back and laughed. "That's a side I didn't see before!"

I rolled my eyes at myself. "I guess I should have warned you."

"Oh, no. No no. This is way more fun." He looked at the kitten in the box. "He's been fed?"

"He was the first one," I said. "Pollux, could you stop licking the kitten, please? It's not a lollypop."

He plunked his ass down and stared up at me balefully. I shook my head. "I'll say this, he's an exceptionally smart dog. He actually listens. We only had barking idiots on the farm."

"Oh, he's a barking idiot." Marcus laughed. "After all he barked at the wall for weeks."

"Yeah, but he was barking at the kittens, so I'll forgive him."

Marcus took the two milk drunk fuzz balls from my arms, placing them in the box. "Let's go get something to eat. I need food, and you do too."

"I need sex."

He laughed, and cupped my chin. "Chase. Make no mistake, I want to sleep with you. But just because we've gotten to the point where your demi isn't an obstacle, doesn't mean we stop getting to know each other."

I hated that he made sense. I just wanted him to fuck me, and soon. It had been way too long since I'd been at this point.

He brushed his lips over mine. "Trust me, Chase.

You will not regret having dinner with me."

"Foodie foreplay?"

Shaking his head ruefully, Marcus looked at me through his lashes. "Why do I have the feeling that I'm going to be really, really sore for work on Monday."

I clapped my hands like an overstimulated seal—I needed to get myself under control—and startled the kittens, who started crying for their mother. I felt *terrible*—for about a minute until Pollux, who looked distressed, climbed into the box and started licking all of them.

"Christ, my dog is going to have a hairball."

MARCUS PICKED an adorable restaurant just north of Washington Square. It was a little, higher end American fusion place I hadn't realized was there, and they were open late. Which was necessary on a Friday night in New York City.

Marcus didn't even open the menu. "I've been coming here way too often after work for a to go order," he admitted. "Now that things have settled in the office, I need to go back to buying and cooking my own food. Mr. Abramovich probably misses me and my hydrant-fouling beast."

"Mr. Abramovich hoses that thing off every day," I answered. "Because your dog isn't the only one *peesseeng* on it. He also hate when dogs takes *sheets* in front of his produce."

"And, he has the best produce," Marcus said. "I can't afford to keep eating out like this. At some point, my food budget is going to outpace my rent."

I nodded. "I've been trying to be good. Pollux has actually helped me. When you were working late and the poor guy needed out, I was always popping into Abramovich's for some veggies and protein that I could whip together really fast. It's been good."

Marcus grabbed my hand. "You have no idea how grateful I am that you were there and willing to walk him. I know Missy has the key, but she has a really bad knee and her walking him would have been too much for her."

"Eh, I like animals." I raised an eyebrow. "Clearly demonstrated by my hysterics over a cat I'd pulled out of a wall less than twenty-four hours earlier."

The waiter poured some wine for us while Marcus laughed. "I'm not much better, you know. I can get pretty hysterical over some pretty dumb stuff."

I studied the light in the wine glass. "But I'll bet you crying over a dead squirrel didn't get you punished."

"Not ever." He nodded. "My dad is a man's man, but he's not about that toxicity. I was raised to be as caring and careful as my sisters. And both of my sisters can beat the tar out of an attacker and change their own oil."

"Nice!" I said, toasting him.

Tapping his glass against mine, we both took a sip. He nodded, clearly liking the wine.

"Your dad?" he asked.

It was easy to tell by the tone of his voice he knew

it was a touchy subject. I stared at my glass, and tried to figure out how to approach that mess. "I'm not the prodigal son," I said. "There would be no fatted calf if I showed up at the front door of their house. Mom keeps trying, but it's not happening. Haven't been home in twelve years. Don't plan on changing that."

"Sounds like a plan." He smiled, and toasted me.

And just like that, I fell for Marcus Romano.

I had already been falling. His patient, kind manner. His willingness to figure out why Pollux was nuts. His sincere apology when he couldn't make it the night we shifted my apartment around. His fun, innocent, non-flirty texts. The nights we spent chatting and eating good or bad take out in the past week.

He really got me. He could tell I wasn't about to give him more than that for a moment in time. We didn't need more than that right now. We were getting to know each other and there was time for deep philosophical questions about our families later.

"Don't you have an audiobook lined up soon?" I asked.

"Oh, I had to ask the author to change the due date on one, because of that mess. But I'm almost caught up with my schedule and I can start on some new projects. I'm taking on a..." He looked around. "Cishet straight romance."

I stage-gasped, "No!"

"Right?" He waggled his eyebrows. "It's a deliciously filthy BDSM story, though, and I had trouble getting through it without a cold shower."

"Did you take the shower?"

"Yes, but it was warm and there was a lot of soap."

I nearly choked on the piece of bread I had just taken a bite of. After a moment to recover, I laughed and shook my head. "I thought *my* newly awakened libido was going to be the problem tonight."

"I'm pretty much constant sexual innuendo if I'm in a good mood," Marcus said. "It's gotten me in trouble. In fact you almost got me in trouble today for smiling at my crotch during the meeting."

"Why...why were you smiling at your crotch?"

"Because you were sitting there."

"Wait..."

"My phone. Before things went bad, I had you perched on my dick so I could feel it when you texted me."

I nodded solemnly. "Better than a Fleshlight."

He choked on the wine this time. "Okay, I deserved that."

The whole meal was like that. Just innuendo after innuendo, and I hadn't laughed that hard in a very long time. Marcus didn't want anything more than for us to eat and get to know each other a little more. It was a relief in a way, because even though I desperately wanted in his pants, he wasn't clawing after the demisexual gay man hoping for a lucky break.

It was so hard to find people like Kieran and Marcus, and that one of them had a spark that attracted me was even better.

Abramovich's store was shut up tight by the time we headed back to the apartments. We headed up the stairs and into my apartment, to check on Pollux and the kittens. They were all sound asleep, but it had been nearly five hours since their last feeding and we had to wake them up.

"I'll take Pollux out for a short walk, and you get all the KMR mixed up. I'll come back and help you feed them," Marcus said, grabbing the dog's leash from the back of the front door.

And sure enough, just about the time I had finished with the formula, he walked back in and the bottles were ready.

"That was a really short walk," I said.

"He just needs to stretch his legs, maybe leave me something I have to scoop and that's about it. He's good about *dark means in.*"

I picked up two of the kittens and handed them to him, then put all four bottles on the table. I picked up the other two kittens and a blanket and got everything arranged to get them on the nipples.

These little balls of fur were too adorable for me. That they were living in a wall with their mother just blew my mind. I wondered how they got in there, and how they would have gotten out. I was happy they were all in good health and that I could help their mother in whatever way I could.

"What time does the vet open in the morning?"

"Nine. They'll be there nine to two, and they'll be

waiting for us," I answered. "Marcus..."

"Let's wait to make any kind of decisions until we hear what the vet found from the tests and scans," he answered my unspoken question. "We just don't know what her condition is and you're going to find I'm ruthlessly optimistic."

I grinned. "I need ruthless optimism sometimes."

"I find it preferable to sitting in the corner, rocking and weeping," he said. "Did that already."

That I filed away for another time. There was a lot to unpack there, and while we were feeding kittens was not the time to do it.

"When we get these guys settled again, would you like to come over to my apartment?"

I must have worn the confusion on my face. *I have a perfectly good bed right there.*

Marcus chuckled lightly. "I can show you my studio. Where I record the books."

"You have a *studio*? I didn't see that when I was in there to pick up Pollux."

"Well, sort of? It's a booth in my bedroom closet, but it's easily disassembled and moved. I designed it to fit in a small space since I knew that New York City wasn't famous for it's large and generous square footage in living abodes."

"Nice." I laughed. "But you seriously record right in your apartment?"

"Yep. I spent a lot of money on good equipment since that's how I was able to move down here." He looked up from the kittens in his lap. "Wanna see it?"

"Yes, of course I do!"

"Cool."

Cool was possibly an understatement. This was Marcus Chastain's recording booth. This was *Marcus'* recording booth.

The kittens had settled and Pollux had no inclination to join us versus snuggling up to those fuzzballs. Marcus huffed and walked away from him, leading me into his own apartment across the way.

He slid the closet door open, and damned if there wasn't a whole studio, just 24 inches deep and 4 feet wide. Leaning in, he turned on a light, and the little soundboard lit up. I could see the microphone, and the comfy chair, and the reading stand. The computer there was a detachable tablet style that clearly got take apart often.

"Wow, this is it?"

"I know it's not much—"

"It is so cool you can get something like this together," I said, waving him off. "It's such a compact little space. But, don't you work at a sound studio?"

"I do." Marcus nodded. "But I don't want to profit off their equipment. It's an ethical line. I'm not up for mixing that. I need that paycheck and I need this one. So, a tiny studio in a closet."

"Brilliant." I smiled.

He sat down in the chair and pulled the boom mike down. Pausing, he considered something and then looked at me standing there. "I was going through a rough read of this one scene...wanna watch?"

"Wait, what?"

"Pull up a chair." He tossed his chin to the one in the corner. "Bring it over. This is all a lot of fun for me."

I nearly ran to grab the chair and pull it in close. With a laugh, he started turning knobs and hitting buttons and booting up the computer. Detaching the tablet, he pulled up the script, and settled it on the reading stand in front of him.

"Okay, this is that dirty book I was telling you about earlier. I've been doing rough reads of the more filthy parts to get a feel for them. I do that first, so if there are words I don't know or can't pronounce or there are editing errors, I can get through those more easily."

He pulled out a bottle of water from under the table and took a drink. "Once I hit the record button, just don't say anything, okay?"

"Got it."

Skimming the page one more time, he took another sip and hit a few buttons. "This is a rough read for *Untied*, Katherine Rhodes, Chapter Thirteen. Mark."

A little button on the board made a clapper sound.

"Kneel," he said.

"Cece brought her hands back and sat up. She slid off the bed and landed on her knees. She nuzzled his hard cock through the leather—the

best way she could think of to ask him to take it out and show her.

He threaded his hands through her hair and pulled her back. "Take them off," he said by way of permission.

She brought her tied hands to his waist and slipped the button out of the fastener. She pulled the zipper down and saw that he was completely naked underneath. She slipped her hands in both directions and pulled the waist of the pants down, slipping it over his erection. He sprang free, and she immediately captured his hard length in her mouth. She wrapped her lips around him and pulled him all the way into her mouth, tasting his pre-cum and playing with his head.

"Oh, Cece," he groaned. "Such a good girl."

She moved him in and out of her puckered lips, tasting him, craving him. She hummed softly around his shaft, and she felt him twitching against her lips. She wanted to taste him in her mouth and was working him, trying to convince him to spill inside. She ran her tongue over the delicate seam on the underside and teased the head.

Jesus H. Tapdancing Christ on a cracker.

His voice was silk on silk. Husky, deeper than his normal speaking tone, the words were nothing but perfection, not a hint of an accent of any sort. They fit the scene perfectly, rough, strong, but caring, and shockwaves of his tone tripped over my skin.

The words flowed, like a smooth fountain of sweet vanilla and chocolate I could dip my finger in and lick the sweetness of his sound from. There was no innuendo, and he left none there—it was pure, unadulterated sex and desire laced into each word.

I smacked my hand on the stop button, turned him in the chair, and slammed my mouth over his. There was no half hard about me. I was fully erect, and fully dressed and one of those didn't belong.

CHAPTER FOURTEEN

MARCUS

WELL THEN.

Not pulling back even a little from the assaulting kiss, I yanked the headphones off and pushed the microphone out of the way.

For just a moment, I toyed with the idea of pulling back and shutting the board down, but *fuck that* because I needed to fuck Chase, *right now*.

Never releasing him from the kiss, I wrapped my hands around his arms, and backed him away from the closet and toward the bed. His arms slipped around me, pressing him close to my chest.

God, he felt good.

He was just a few inches shorter than me and the difference made it so easy to lean down and capture his lips over and over. He tasted like wine and chocolate, the remains of the fabulous meal we'd had.

I hadn't meant to seduce him by reading that

erotica, but he was clearly taken by whatever it was he heard there. It was just a stage voice I used, but I could feel his erection long and hot, low on my hip.

"You're sure?" I whispered, flicking open the buttons on his shirt.

"Just tell me you have lube and condoms," he answered.

"Nightstand," I answered. "Hope springs eternal."

He nipped at my lip, let me finish unbuttoning the casual blue shirt he'd put on.

Chase's hand landed on his chest. "Hope springs eternal? What does that mean?"

"It's been a really, really, *really* long time since I've had a hot guy in my bed." I lifted an eyebrow. "Major cockblock is living with your parents."

He laughed. "Okay, cowboy, pony up. Get naked and let me see what the rest of the homosexual population has been missing out on."

"But half the fun is undressing you..."

"Not if I'm going to blow my load just because you touched my dick," he stated. "Which is totally what's about to happen if you don't back up and shuck the clothes."

I leaned in very close to his lips and breathed the words across them, "Schuck. How every midwestern of you. I kind of like it."

The shiver ran through him, and he closed his eyes. "I will not come, I will not come, I will not come."

"No, not until I'm buried deep in your ass."

"Oh, shit, oh fuck," Chase gasped. "Bedroom voice. Very dangerous. Very orgasmic. Very climaxy."

At no point in all the books I had recorded had it occurred to me that my *voice* could be the very thing that got someone off. But Chase clearly associated my clean reading voice with *sex*, because he had a collection of them with bookmarks at the dirty parts.

I was back at his shirt and I unfastened the buttons, just three left and then quickly popped open the cuffs. Pulling the whole thing off and and his t-shirt over his head, I had him standing there, barechested in a moment.

"You're absolutely sculpted perfection," I said, using *that voice*. I leaned down and ran my tongue from just below his ear, down his throat to the soft skin of his collar. "Your skin is perfect, and warm, and soft and—"

"*Fuck*, Marcus, I'm only just hanging on here."

I reached down and rubbed my hand over the bulge of his erection. "Mm, nice and hard."

"Jeee*sus*."

I dropped to my knees and brushed my cheek over him, nuzzling the outline of his dick. It had been a very long time since I'd hooked up, and even longer since I had a boyfriend. I hadn't been kidding when I said that Mom and Dad were a total cockblock.

Chase's fingers slipped through my hair and I tipped my chin up to stare into those magnificent blue eyes. I didn't let them go, even as my hand found the button and zipper of his pants, and I relieved him of his clothes. My hands skimmed his pants and his boxers down off his waist, down his legs, feeling the rough scrape of hair on them, and outlining the muscles I could feel dancing just below the skin of his thighs.

I still held his gaze as my hand slipped back up his leg, over his stomach and wrapped my hand around the base of his cock. I leaned in, finally pulling my eyes from his and inhaled the scent of the downy, soft hair at the base, slipping one hand to his balls.

"Marcus, I can't..."

"You totally can, baby, you totally can."

I licked a stripe up the underside of him, pausing to collect the pre-cum that had gathered there. I flicked my tongue over the slit and I felt his cock twitch hard.

Looking up once more and locking my eyes with his, I slipped my lips over his wide crown, and swallowed him right down to the root.

He shouted an inarticulate sound, and if I hadn't grabbed his ass seconds before, he would have fallen down. I spun us around, never letting his cock escape my lips, and pushed him down on the bed so he wouldn't fall.

Flopping back, he gasped, "Jesus Christ, Marcus!"

Pulling off him a bit, I swirled my tongue around the shaft, delighted at his girth. He was hard and hot and heavy and the wonderful taste of male that I loved so much.

I wrapped my fingers around his base again. I knew he was close to coming, but I wanted to play a little more before he did. It was fun. He was squirming and kicking and trying desperately not to squirm and kick.

"Oh, God, Marcus. Shit, shit!" Chase gasped when I pulled him back in and sucked hard on him.

Letting him pop out of my mouth, I put a hand on his stomach. "Sit up, Chase. Watch me suck you."

He gasped and was up on his elbows in a flash. He found my eyes, and I saw his were a whirling pool of lust. I gathered a taste of his precum again, then slowly slid his length into my mouth. I could see him gasping for air and trying not to break our locked gaze.

Moving my hand from the base of his dick, I cradled and fondle the heavy sac below. My finger grazed over the thin strip of super sensitive skin that led to his hole, and I saw a shock of pained delight pass over his face. Chase sat up a little further and skimmed his fingers through my hair, trying to pull me off.

"You have to stop, Marcus. You have to. I'm going to come if you don't."

I hummed in the back of my throat and he squealed from the feeling it created. Reaching up, I pinched one of his pointed, willing nipples, eliciting another screech.

"Marcus! I can't stop this!"

That was just fine with me. I moved my mouth up and down his length faster, pulling and pushing against the fingers in my hair. Chase got the message when I caught his eyes again.

His breath caught, and he tightened his grip. "You want my cum? Down your throat?"

God, yes. I did my best to nod, and it seemed to just set him off. He jacked his hips up and his cock hit the back of my throat. I gagged a bit, and then—

"Oh, *shit*, yes!" Chase's fingers pulled on my hair painfully as he erupted in my mouth, spilling his climax deep in my throat. I immediately swallowed, then pulled back a little so I could taste him on my tongue. When the next pulse of cum hit my mouth, I knew I was addicted to his flavor.

When the orgasm released him, he flopped back on the bed. "Jesus, God, and all the angels in Heaven." He picked his head up just enough to look at me with my chin on his thigh, smiling at him. "That was illegally good."

"Once upon a time, yeah, it was illegal. I think they jailed Oscar Wilde for being flagrantly gay."

"He was a dandy, and sentenced to hard labor for gross indecency," Chase said. "Please come up here and kiss me, Marcus. I'm pretty sure I can't move right now."

I kissed my way up his naked body. "Odd fact to know."

"My drama teacher in England loved Wilde." His breath was still heavy, and reacting to each touch of my lips. "He loved *The Importance of Being Earnest.* He was also, himself, a 'dandy'."

Humming as I reached his neck, I couldn't help but chuckle a bit. "Oh? Did we have a bit of a taboo relationship, Chase?"

He laughed hard. "The dude fucked me in the bathroom of the Old Vic. It was more than a *bit* of a taboo relationship."

"Note to self, Chase likes dirty encounters in intellectual settings." I snagged the drawer handle and pulled it open, lifting out the condoms and lube. "Right now though, we need to have a dirty encounter right here."

"You're still fully dressed," Chase hissed. "Get naked, you magnificent cocksucker."

"Oh, you liked that, eh?"

"I'm demi, not dead."

I slowly licked at his lips and tasted his smile. "I don't know, man, you're kind of boneless. Oh!" His hand wrapped around my still mostly hard dick through my pants and made me gasp.

"I think you can solve my boneless problem." His words dusted over my cheek as he moved to suckle my ear. "I want this in my ass, Marcus. Please."

"So polite," I answered, reaching out for the bottle of lube. "Get on the bed the right way, Chase, and maybe you'll get just that."

"Will you be naked?"

"Oh yes, baby." I gripped his neck and whispered in The Voice, "I plan to be fully naked, fully erect, just so I can feel every inch of your perfect body and your hard length against my skin as I drive this cock into you."

Chase's eyes rolled back in his head. "Jesus

Christ, Marcus." The bright baby blues popped open again. "Not tonight, but one night, I want to see if you can make me come with just your voice."

"Mmm. Challenge accepted."

Scrambling out from under me, Chase slipped up the bed and leaned against my headboard. "Strip. I want to see you strip and I want to see you naked and I want to see you back in this bed."

"Bossy bottom," I quipped, pulling my shirt up and over my head.

"Sometimes, maybe." His grin was wicked, and he canted his head. "Sometimes, I might like to be the bossy top."

"Mmm, I don't mind switching." My dick twitched in agreement. Yeah, definitely could handle that with Chase and that magnificent cock of his. Unbuttoning my pants and slipping them off my hips, and down my legs, I grinned at him. "But not tonight."

His eyes went wide, and he grinned like he'd won the biggest prize at a carnival game "Oh. Damn. I'll shut up if that's what I get all the time."

I leaned over the bed and crawled over him. "Oh, don't worry about shutting up. I have just the tool to help you with that."

"Ohyesmyyes."

He pushed forward from the headboard and pressed his lips to mine. "I want to explore every line and dip in your body with my tongue, Marcus. But not tonight. Please, please, fuck me?"

"How do you want it, babe?" I asked, smoothing

my hand up and down his hip.

"Hard, fast, deep."

Chuckling, I kissed him again. "Well, that's a given, but do you want to face me, or do you want me to pound your ass into the mattress, face first."

"Both please." He grinned. "Like this, facing you. I want to see your O-face. I want to see what you look like when you spill yourself inside me."

Kneeling, I gripped his hips and pulled him down the bed. A gasp of shock escaped him, and then a laugh. "Shit, Marc, is sex supposed to be this much fucking fun?"

"It's supposed be fun fucking..." I slanted my mouth across his and possessed him. I licked over his lips, and when he parted them, I slipped my tongue across his and a deep, thrilling moan erupted from him.

He was absolutely delicious. Everything he did spoke to me, or answered me without words. I had not been able to get him off my mind since the floor incident last night and now, here in this bed with him, I didn't want to.

I wanted more Chase Garcia. More and more.

I popped the cap open on the bottle of lube and knelt back. Chase handed me a pillow and I slipped it under his hips as he wrapped his hands behind his own knees and pulled himself up and open.

Putting just a few drops on my finger, I dusted over his hole, and he let out a groan from deep inside. "Oh, my God, it's been s-so long..."

He arched his back as my finger breached him. I was slow and careful—if it really had been that long, I didn't want to hurt him at all. And I knew there was a burn.

I felt the instant he relaxed and started to slide my finger in and out. I pulled all the way out, slicked two fingers this time, and slipped back in. He was tight—but what was I expecting? He admitted a long time and with all of the reading I'd done over the past few days about demiromance and demisexuality, it should not have surprised me at all.

It did delight me though.

"Oh, shit," Chase managed. "That's amazing, *ohhh*!"

The *oh* jumped out of him as I found the magic button inside of him—his prostate. His flagging erection suddenly stopped flagging and started pointing again. Up at me, and as I teased him, further until it reached a tipping point and laid itself against his skin, angry, purpling, and ready for a tug or two. I twisted and opened my fingers, eventually adding more lube and a third finger for just a few thrusts before I pulled them away completely.

"Dick, dick, get your dick in me," Chase panted.

I liked this slightly out of control, finally horny man demanding I slide myself inside him.

I rolled the condom on quickly and slicked myself up with some more lube. I didn't know how long I was going to last—I'd been ignoring my own hard-on in favor of prepping him, and I enjoyed that part a lot.

So did my cock, and I was very hard and ready for this.

Before I could do anything, he grabbed my sheathed erection and pressed me against his hole. "Come on, please. Please."

"Bossy!" I swatted his ass and he cried out.

"I'm begging—*shit*!"

The tip of my shaft popped through the ring of his ass, and there was an immense sense of satisfaction between the two of us. I pushed, slowly, feeling every inch of myself nestling deeper inside, and finally, I bottomed out and my own eyes rolled back in my head.

"Damn, Chase, you feel so good."

"Don't move yet, don't move. If you move, I'll come."

"Again."

He let go of his legs but hooked them around my back. His palms skimmed over my arms, my shoulders, down my flanks, and back up over my chest. Catching my mouth with his, he kissed me hard, possessing me this time.

"Can you move?"

I nodded against his lips.

"Good." He smiled. "Fuck me."

I really hadn't meant to give Chase all the ammunition to forge this connection. I was hoping he'd be a friend. A hot, sexy friend, but I had been fine stopping there.

Now, though, dick deep in him, there was so much more I wanted from him. He was sweet, funny, helpful, kind, and hot. His cute pajamas, his amazing outfits, his smooth golden skin, his dark hair and blue eyes. And now, his handsome features, blissed out on sex and lust and I was falling hard for this guy.

Shuttling in and out, keeping a slow pace at first, I realized that I was finally in a place—and a man—I wanted more time with. I wanted to explore what we could be. I needed to explore this. After all the shit I had been through, after all I had done, and how I had kept myself away from people...here was Chase.

"Hard, baby," he gasped. "Hard."

Not a problem. I didn't move faster, but I bottomed out every time, pressing over his prostate. He was grunting and his nails were digging into my shoulders.

"God, yes, Chase, mark me," I managed. I wanted those bruises on my shoulder, those crescent marks from his nails.

One hand disappeared to wrap around his own cock, and he slicked his hand up and down his length.

"Good boy," I managed. "Make yourself come. Take your pleasure. I want to see your cum on your chest."

He sucked in a breath, and nodded. "Yes."

I shifted my hips and nailed his spot every time I drove in, and he started having trouble catching his breath. "I'm not coming until you do," I managed to instruct. His passage was so tight around my cock—it made my brain short circuit. He pulsed hard around me, a sign he was ready to come, and my eyes almost went crossed. I needed him to come soon or I wasn't going to be able to hold back.

"Marcus!"

A shout, and twist of his features, and his seed shot from the tip of his cock, up onto his chest. His passage tightened on me and there was no holding back—I immediately filled the condom between us with my own release in just a few hard thrusts into him.

"Damn."

CHAPTER FIFTEEN

CHASE

I COULDN'T SEE. THE ORGASM RENDERED me blind and deaf.

Well, maybe not deaf. There was a ringing in my ears and I could hear a soft chuckle above me.

Marcus slipped out of me and I felt his movements telegraphed through the mattress as he disposed of the condom and put the lube back on the nightstand.

Panting hard, I tried to find my center again, but before I could, I felt a pair of lips and a tongue licking and sucking their way up from my once-again-exhausted cock, over my navel, up my abs.

Cracking one eye open, I found the man who had made me so boneless, again, cleaning my cum off my body.

"Jesus, Marc... That's so fucking sexy. But, please stop because I just don't think that my balls can handle another orgasm right now."

"Just cleaning up after you." I felt his smile on my skin.

"Get up here and kiss me." I tugged on his arms and pulled him up.

Normally, I didn't go for the whole 'taste your own spunk' kink, but on Marcus' lips and tongue, it was different. Probably because it was him and there was a whole lot I liked about him.

He pulled me against his side and let out a satisfied sigh as he made himself comfortable. "You're going to be sore in the morning, Chase."

"Fuck, I hope so," I answered. "Because I seriously don't want to forget that fucking."

"You like pineapple." His voice was sleepy.

"I do," I answered.

"You taste like it." He laughed. Sitting up, he looked around like he had never seen this room before. "We should shower." He slipped off the bed and wandered buck naked into the bathroom.

Man, that ass.

"Shower in the morning," I called to him.

He reappeared with a washcloth and walked back to my side of his bed. "Agreed. But, gotta clean off the sex residue. Sexidue."

"Cum cakes," I mumbled.

"Spunktacular."

I was laughing as he carefully wiped between my legs, brushing over my wonderfully sore hole. "I honestly have never had this much fun during sex."

I really hadn't. Not ever, not with my first boyfriend, the naughty professor, or the last long-term disaster I was in. No one made me laugh while we were in the act.

"Sex is a ridiculous action," Marcus said, and swiped the last of my release off my stomach. He tossed the washcloth just inside the door of the bathroom. "I mean male-male or male-female, you're stuffing normally squishy parts into squishy holes and making your brain do weird things expressing its delight in all this temporarily hard stuff inside squishy holes."

I couldn't stop laughing at that. He settled himself against me, a little laugh escaping him as well.

"If you can't have fun doing something fun, why bother?"

I rested my head in the crook of his shoulder. "Is that your life motto?"

"No, that's *what the hell is going on right now for real*?"

I chuckled again. "Pollux and the kittens are in my apartment. Should we get them?"

"Do you want to just sleep there?"

"As long as you're next to me naked, I don't care."

Had I really just said that? Wow. This was a lot for my poor 'people suck' brain to absorb. I didn't like that my whole modus operandi seemed to be *all in* or *all out*, with no in between.

Once I'd realized I was demiromantic, it was a lot easier to deal with not lusting after people like most of my friends did. Hookups, one-night stands, short term relationships were not on my radar. If I didn't have an emotional, intellectual relationship, my libido just wasn't interested. I couldn't get excited over random sex.

A blessing and a curse. Kieran had been one of the few men who had been willing to try and form that connection, and I had found him on a dating site that was a little less popular and lot less sticky than Grindr.

Before that, had been the three year mess with Hans that had imploded badly. So badly it had been years until I could recover part of my property from him in a civil suit. So badly, none of our mutual friends remained mutual, and none of the ones who sided with him could convince him to give me so much as a pair of underwear.

So badly that after he lost the civil case, he moved back to Austria and I think changed his name. which was better for all parties involved. Self-absorbed fucker.

And Logan. Who I'd fallen in love with, and he then just as quickly fallen out of love with me. He'd tried to drag me into a poly relationship with him and the new guy, but he was using it as an excuse to keep a place to live and cheat on me right under my nose.

I might like some kink, but being cuckolded was not one of them.

"What if Pollux has to pee?" I finally asked.

"Potty patch," he grumbled half awake.

"That's in here." I had already started to get off the bed. We couldn't leave the animals in the other apartment.

"Ugh, shit you're right," Marcus said, tossing a hand over his eyes.

Leaning over him in the bed, I pressed a kiss to his lips. "Be right back, *voce.*"

Pollux was still curled up around his kittens in the box, and once I convinced him to walk, I moved everyone into the other apartment and got them settled.

Five minutes later I was tucked into Marcus and sound asleep.

MY BONER was poking Marcus's ass. It was distinctly not a pee-hard-on. It was well and truly morning wood, and I was pretty sure that Marcus was not awake, yet.

Which meant I could think of ways to wake him up. My still sleep addled brain was working way better than it should be at that point.

Nestling closer to him, I slipped my erection between his cheeks, and slid it back and forth, nudging his taint at the far end. I wrapped a hand around his hip and found that I wasn't the only one suffering with morning wood.

I paused to grab the lube and quickly slicked my fingers and my erection and chucked it behind me. I slowly started moving again, bumping over his hole and nudging against his sac. My other hand was around his dick, following the rhythm of my movements behind him.

"Mmm," Marcus mumbled. "That's nice."

"Just stay," I murmured in his ear.

Another contented hum slipped out of him and he pressed his head back toward me. I kept a slow and steady pace, both with my hand and cock. He felt so damn good pressed against me, in my hand, over my erection.

I felt his body tremble a few minutes later, and his breath was more a gasp than anything else.

"Want to come," he whispered.

My other hand wasn't busy at the moment, and I snaked it down his back, to the top of his ass and slowly further, reaching for his hole and brushing against it, over it a few times. Marcus' whole body shook, and I felt his shaft jerk in my hand. I held him just a little bit tighter, and as I brushed over him again, the tip of my cock pressing against his balls, he let out a sigh of relief and I felt him shoot his release into the sheets.

He pressed his thighs together when he recovered, and gave my cock a tighter place to slide through. I pressed my dick in harder against him with the hand that had just jerked him off and in a just few pumps later, I came.

My cum spread on his thighs and ass, but he let out a satisfied breath, then rolled over. He leaned over and gave me a long, sensual kiss. "Morning, baby. I think there's a shower in our future."

"And a load of laundry," I teased.

"Well, yes. I'll strip the bed if you get the shower going."

I tried to spring out of bed, but it didn't work very well. My foot got caught on the dog at the side of the bed and I went down, dragging all the sheets with me. Pollux woofed indignantly as the sheets covered and trapped him.

"Shit, the kittens." Marcus popped off the bed with ease after I had taken the sheets out.

He trotted into the living room, buck naked, covered with my release which did funny, primitive things to me—and damn that was a nice *good morning* for me, and laughed loudly.

"Chase, the kittens are learning to climb." The amusement in his voice was undeniable.

I grabbed my boxers and slipped myself out of the sheets and into them. Snagging his, I walked over and handed them to Marcus.

The kittens had definitely learned to climb.

There was one hanging on the curtains on the window. Another had managed to get to the top of the bookcase. The last two were perched on a shelf above the couch.

Pollux barked and walked into the room. He sat down and barked again. Marcus shook his head, pulling his boxers on. "Well, let's get them down. Then you can run the shower and I'll join you quickly because you jump started the bed stripping."

"I can jump start—"

His hand covered my mouth. "Shh. Shush. Keep those ideas for the shower."

"Ooh, really?" I asked, walking into the living room, and heading for the curtains.

"It's Saturday. The vet opens at nine, and it's just past eight now," he answered, heading for the bookshelf. "Keep your ideas for the shower."

We were almost late for the consultation.

CHAPTER SIXTEEN

MARCUS

One month later...

"MC!" CHASE CHIRRUPED WALKING INTO his apartment.

I laughed, watching Pollux play fighting with Proust as MC sat on the back of the couch. Chase walked straight to her and she looked up at him. "Mrrrow?"

"How's my baby kitty?" Chase scooped her up and cradled her against his shoulder.

"I'm good, mister human." I mimicked a high-pitched kitty-ish voice. "I have shat in the proper place today, and didn't break the skin on other mister human's finger when he gave me my pills."

He lifted an eyebrow. "Do you really think she sounds like that?"

"She's a cat, Chase, she sounds like a cat. Some meowing, a few purrs, the occasional hiss, and gets scared by her own farts."

"Hmph." He turned and walked into his now-back to normal bedroom, making soothing sounds at his cat.

I shook my head and went back to stirring my risotto.

Two minutes later, he appeared in a light T-shirt, cargo shorts and no shoes, with MC following him back into the kitchen. "What did the vet have to say?"

"She's fine," I answered. "He's thrilled with her results, and we just need to keep an eye on the incision and make sure it's looking as good as it did today. Her blood came back perfect, and she's even gained a half a pound, which made him unreasonably happy. He wants two more weekly checks and then we can go to a month."

"And the other kittens?"

"I'm bringing Tarzan to Sorcha tomorrow. Princess and Bubbles are settling in with their new home perfectly." I leaned over, and stared straight into his eyes. "Everything is fine, babe. Don't stress. All the animals are perfectly fine."

I was forever grateful that MC's cancer had turned out to be a slow growing, self-contained tumor that the doctor was able to cut right out. She'd had some chemo to make sure that it was out of her system, and she was home with Chase. None of it was cheap, but Chase had a huge network of friends who chipped in and helped us pay for her care.

I was being sucked into the circle. I'd give Chase shit for all his friends, but I didn't mind hanging around with all likeminded guys and girls in the group.

"Did you hear from Felix?"

While I had never met the guy, the story of his arrogance and ridiculous over the top actions had caught my attention. But more, we were actually puzzled by him.

"I haven't heard a thing. Just that his FMLA has another six weeks on it, and then he had to either come back or take whatever position they have for him." Chase folded his arms and leaned back on the counter. "I am actually worried about him, and can't even begin to think of what could be going on."

"Could be rehab," I answered.

"No. I mean, I don't *think* it's that. He never seemed the type to be into the nose candy. I hope he comes back soon. I'm tired of doing his work and the client is getting impatient with my *different style than Felix* attitude." He snorted. "Yelling at me doesn't do anything, buddy. Every artist is different."

"Man, tell me about that," I mumbled.

"How's the big contract coming?" He smiled, cuddling MC who had perched on his shoulder.

"Everything is rolling along." I smiled. "We'll have the first five episodes done next week. I am really thrilled at how they are coming out."

The very pit of my stomach flipped. I'd been warned today that Roberts was going to be in, and I was glad I wasn't wasting a vacation day. But three times in the last month, he'd violated the rider—not just violated it, but somehow managed to wander into the large editing room Sorcha and I were working in.

She'd screamed at him to get out. He did. But somehow he'd managed to get back in when she wasn't there. I had to grab my bag and leave before he said a word. I didn't want to be the one running away from him, but I had no choice. There was law involved.

I hadn't told Chase about the whole thing, because that meant I would have to explain everything to him, and I wasn't ready to revisit that yet. I was going to have to, soon, because I realized I wanted Chase to be the real thing for me.

Everything that had happened in the past month felt so very real to me. He was just this expanding ball of personality. He loved the cats, and he loved Pollux and I could just spend hours and hours with him.

I did, in fact. Either in his place or mine. We had defiled just about every surface and cushion in both apartments. The sex was just amazing, and so were the calm mornings with coffee and croissants. I also thought it was time to have the conversation. We were sleeping in each other's beds almost every night, anyway.

I just had no idea how to approach the "move in with me" conversation. I'd never ever had to think about it before. And I didn't know if just two months was really enough.

"Well, thank you for taking MC to the vet today."

"You know he loves her." I smiled. "He's always happy to see a happy ending for a street cat."

"That he is," Chase said. "I wonder how he makes

any money to stay in business."

"Because there are people like Mrs. Colmanetti who call him all hours of the day asking about Mimi's hang nail."

"It's Marguerite Magnificent. Not Mimi."

I leveled a gaze at him, and he cracked up laughing. "Okay, fine. Point taken."

I cleared my throat. "So. I was thinking."

Bang! Bang! Bang!

That was one of the most threatening knocks I'd ever heard. And I had been on the wrong end of police knocks. I looked at Chase, who seemed confused.

"You weren't expecting anyone?" I asked.

"No...are they looking for you maybe?"

"Shit, I hope not," I mumbled.

He headed over the door, putting MC back on her perch at the back of the couch. The *bang!* came again, and he hesitated to pull it open.

"Don't wait," I said. "If the cops want in, they'll break the door."

"Cops?" His eyes snapped to mine.

"Mistaken identity, or bad address," I said. "Not that I think you're dealing drugs or committing felonies."

"Right."

He peeked through the peephole and gasped. I saw his hand tighten on the door, but not actually move to open it.

"Chase?"

They banged on the door again.

He finally seemed to come out of his trance and

yanked the door open before there was another bang. The person on the other side had their hand up as if they were going to do just that.

"Rider." There was nothing nice or polite about my boyfriend's voice at that moment. "What the fuck are you doing here?"

"I'm here to find you."

"Well, you found me. Now fuck off and lose my address."

He went to slam the door, but Rider—whoever the hell he was—put his hand out and slammed it back open. "I don't fucking want to be here, gay boy. So you're gonna hear me out."

I cleared my throat and folded my arms. I was a big man, and I wasn't afraid to use that to defend Chase. "Rethink your words right now, *Rider*, or I'll make sure you forget this address."

"Holy shit..." He stepped back and his eyes traveled up my body, finally reaching my hair.

"Do I meet your approval?"

His eyes snapped back to Chase. "Is that...is he..."

"Rider, this my boyfriend, Marcus. Marcus, this is my brother, Rider."

Brother. *Well.*

"You really shacked up with a...guy?"

"We aren't shacked up," Chase said. "What the hell are you doing here?"

He stared at Chase for a moment and then sighed. "Can I come in?"

"Are you going to dislocate my shoulder again?"

"I don't want to be here, Chase. At all. I hate the

city, I dislike your lifestyle choice, and I have a life back in Illinois I'd like to get back to."

He let go of the door and walked back toward the kitchen. Rider was a good six inches shorter than me, but his stank attitude made up for it. I watched him walk into the living room and slammed the door behind him.

MC sniffed at him and walked out of the room into the bedroom. She meowed once and Proust and Pollux came running after her.

Ha. Cat had good taste and sense.

I followed behind him into the kitchen where Chase had pulled out three beers and handed one to me, smacking the other on the table.

Rider seemed to get the idea quickly, and sat down. I slipped myself behind Chase and rested one hand on his shoulder, letting him know I was there, and held the beer in the other. He leaned back a bit against me.

"Talk, Rider. The sooner you do—"

"You have to come home."

He snorted. "I have to do no such thing. Twelve years since you helped literally throw me out the door nothing but my high school backpack and the clothes I was wearing. I had to beg Mom to give me my bank book and my passport! I slept in a barn overnight and waited for you assholes to leave so I could ask for what was mine."

"You need to come home," he repeated.

"Maybe you didn't hear me—"

"Dad's dying."

There was a heartbeat of silence. Chase folded his arms. "So?"

"He wants to talk to you."

"I have a phone."

"Come on, Chase! He wants to see you one last time before he goes. He's dying. He's got less than six months to live. Can't you give him this?"

"Give him what? The chance to yell at me? To threaten me with conversion therapy? To tell me in person that I'm not his son, and I deserve every bad thing that ever happened to me?"

Rider took a drink from the bottle. "I don't want you to come back. I don't. But this is all Dad has talked about. You won't answer your phone, you won't return messages, and I had absolutely no choice but to come here and see you. I don't care. You're dead to me, choosing to be gay. But Dad...I care about him. I want to see him happy. And making him happy right now means talking to you. In person."

Chase took a drink of his beer. "How long do I have to think about this?"

"He's dying!"

"Six months you said?"

"Jesus, Chase."

He leaned up from me. "Get this straight, right now, *Brother*. You heaved me out the front door after that shit of a mayor's son came and told you I tried to make a move on him. I never, ever, never did. You never asked my side of the story. You and Dad just wanted the fag out of the house. You didn't even *know* I was gay until Jarrit showed up bitching that I had tagged his ass. And this is the reason why I never came out to you." Taking a deep breath, he leaned back against me. "So yes. I get time to think about whether I want to grant my father his dying wish because he couldn't even give me my dignity as a human."

Rider sipped the beer again, thinking. "Do you think you'll need a long time?"

"Are you for real?" he asked.

"I was coming to get you and go right back home," Rider said. "I have no interest in being here longer than I have to."

"Afraid you might catch the gays?" I lifted an eyebrow.

"You people are disgusting."

I bit my tongue. There was nothing good going to come out of my mouth.

"I need time to think. And I would never go back in the same car as you, Rider. Not in a million years." Chase rubbed his hand up and down his arm. "You can stay here overnight because I know you can't afford a hotel in the city—and won't try to find one, or you can turn around and leave right now. Either way, I won't be riding with you."

"If I stay here, where are you sleeping?"

He cocked his head. "At my boyfriend's. Across the hall."

"You share a bed?"

"Seriously? Do you share one with your wife?"

"Yeah, but like...we're not gay."

I blinked a few times. "I'm not even sure what the

hell that means."

"It's not natural."

I was pretty sure I sprained my eyes rolling them. "You can crash here. Or you can leave. But one thing is for sure. Stop making idiotic homophobic comments like that. We're gay, it doesn't spread like ebola. You're not going to suddenly want to hump every male you see."

"You shared...*Chase's* bed?"

I merely lifted an eyebrow.

"Ew."

"We're normal healthy males with a pretty good sex drive," Chase said. "And we don't owe you our sexual history."

Rider chugged the beer. "I'm not staying. Answer your fucking phone. I'm heading back to Illinois and you can either show up for your dying father or not. Either way, I am done with you."

"I was done with you a long time ago." Chase nodded.

Rider slammed the beer bottle on the table and headed for the door. Neither of us moved to see him out, and the door slammed a moment later.

In the next heartbeat, Chase had his face buried in my neck, and I could feel the sobs racking his body. I wrapped my arms around him, and just held him against me. It took him a good long few minutes to start to calm down.

"No time limit," I whispered. "Just breathe for me."

His breath was short, more gasps than breaths at

first, but slowly, as I ran my hand up and down his back, his breathing started to normalize.

"Sorry," he whispered.

"No," I answered. "Absolutely not. Sorry is not allowed. You did nothing wrong. Your brother just barged into your life after...twelve years?, and there's no reason to be sorry."

"I cannot believe he showed up here!" Chase's voice went from upset to indignant. "How dare he? Just invite himself back into my life after all this time! It doesn't work that way! He doesn't get to come back and treat me like shit and think that I'm going kowtow to him!"

I nodded. "You're right. You don't have to do anything you don't want to."

"I didn't get a single call from him. I never got a voice mail. And I know they have the right number because my mother has called me on and off for the past twelve years. So he is a liar, and I don't know what he thinks he's trying to accomplish."

"He seems like every other homophobe I've ever met," I answered. "They think you are less than human and by deigning to come into your life again he has somehow made you better. Toxic hyper-masculinity."

"Is he fucking crying?"

I whipped my head up to see Rider standing in the doorway of the kitchen. I pulled Chase behind me. "Who the fuck let you back in?"

"Door was open—"

"You just fucking walked out! In this part of the

world, you always knock and ask permission. And right now, you do not have permission to be in here!"

He threw something on the table. "For the record, the only people in town who ever want to see your face again are Mom and Dad. Everyone else is perfectly happy having the town fag gone for good."

"*Get out!*"

"Fuck you, cocksucker," he snapped.

I stepped forward and drew up to my full height. "Would you like me to show you how good I am at that? Because, honey, I'll have you screaming my name in a under a minute."

He ran. I was surprised there wasn't cartoon dust behind him as he fled.

I heard a sob-chuckle from behind me, and turned back to Chase leaning against the counter, a hand over his mouth. He was wiping tears from his eyes while he was trying not to laugh. "Honey?"

I chuckled too. "Sometimes, I play the gay card."

"Well, *honey*, you can make me scream your name any time," Chase said, grabbing the envelope on the table. "Lock the door?"

With a grunt, I hurried to the door before the shithead reappeared. Chase was standing next to the kitchen table holding the contents of the envelope in his hand.

Pictures, and a short note.

Chase,
I have no idea if your brother can convince you to come back, but I thought you might

**want these pictures before I throw them out. I
don't want to, but I don't know what to do with
them anymore.**
Mom

And in his hand were dozens of pictures of baby
Chase, from birth to high school. Him and his father,
his mother, his brother. Candids from parties,
summers, holidays, first day of school.

"These are all freshly printed," he whispered.
"Mom had a digital camera from when we were little.
She printed these off."

"To manipulate you?"

"I...I don't think so. I think she did it to remind
me." He looked up and there were tears in his deep
blue eyes. "I don't need to be reminded. I never ever
forgot them."

I pulled out the phone in my pocket.

Marcus: *Dad. I need a favor.*
Daaaad: *What's up, Son?*
Marcus: *We need someone to watch the
animals and can we borrow a car? Family
emergency.*
Daaaad: *One of us will be down tomorrow.*

CHAPTER SEVENTEEN

CHASE

DAWN ROMANO FOLDED HER ARMS around me and pulled me into a tight hug.

"Chase, I'm so glad I finally got to meet you. I wish this could be a better time," she said.

I could feel her sincerity in my very bones, and since I had been an emotional wreck anyway for the past eighteen hours, my brain decided it was fine to start crying.

Again.

"Oh, Chase," she whispered.

"Mrs. Romano—"

"It's Dawn, darling," she said.

"I'm sorry I'm such a mess, Dawn," I said. "I don't know how to feel about any of this."

"Don't try to figure that out right now," she said. "You'll have plenty of time to do that on the drive and while you're there."

"Are you sure you're going to be okay with all these animals?"

"*Psht.* Whatever," she said, waving me off. "We have three dogs, four cats, and chickens. Damn chickens. Thanks to Christy's new abandoned hobby." She looked around the apartment. "At least I won't have to hear that fucking rooster every morning."

I choked. Marcus' mother *swore.*

"So, I'll be sleeping in my son's place, but since he seems to have no ability to decorate, or hell, even purchase furniture, I'll probably be over here most of the time. Are you all right with that?"

"I can't say no—"

"You most certainly can," she said.

"I don't want to say no," I amended with a smile, smearing the remains of the tears off my cheeks.

She nodded. "Do either of the cats need special care?"

"No, just a *lot* of petting. Proust can get very kitteny."

"Pollux still for his twice a day minimum walks?"

"Yes, and a quick pee break before bed."

She smiled and took a quick peek in the cabinets. "I hope you don't mind. Since I'll be over here and my son still eats off paper plates in his place..."

"Of course," I answered. I really should have been offended by this woman coming in here and taking over, nosing through my cabinets, opening my fridge, but I was not. Not in the least.

"What time will Marcus be here?"

"Just about five-thirty," I answered.

"You're driving tonight?"

"First thing in the morning." I cleared my throat. "So, Marcus will just crash on the couch tonight and we'll—"

"Why?" Dawn cocked her head and looked at him.

"Why...what?"

"Why would my son sleep on the couch?"

"Because...you're taking the bed...and..."

She smirked. "And you have a single bed?"

I choked again. "What?"

Pulling out two coffee mugs, she set about making the brew. "I graduated high school in 1979, Chase. I graduated college in 1983. I know all about sex. More, I know all about unmarried sex."

"Holy TMI," I mumbled.

"And if my son hasn't gotten to know you *in the Biblical sense*, and make it worth your while, you walk away from him, you hear me?"

I wasn't sure I could stop choking on the air—it was all me trying not to laugh and die from embarrassment at the same time. "The Biblical sense? Don't they always say that God hates—"

"*Figs*, Chase. God hates figs."

The laugh bubbled out of me and I didn't want to stop it. There was absolutely no doubt in my mind why Marcus was the way he was. This woman was amazing, and whether he and I hung on and made it work, I wanted this kind of acceptance in my life.

"Okay, fine," I said. "Marcus will crash with me. The animals can hang here, and this actually works better because we won't wake you up. Are you sure that you're okay with us taking the car?"

"I have his hostage upstate, so if he crashes, eh. I get the Shelby."

My eyebrow shot up. "He has a Shelby?"

"Fully restored 1965 with his grandfather," she said. "Metallic blue with a white racing stripe."

My mouth fell open. "I had no idea!"

"That's our insurance policy when he borrows one of ours. He can't drive that to Illinois, so he borrows my Camry for the trip." Dawn smiled and poured two mugs of coffee. "Works for me, I don't mind driving the Shelby. Sexy ass car."

"Ohgod,   pleasedon'ttellme   youanddad defiledmycar?"

Marcus was standing in the doorway with a hand over his eyes. Dawn lifted the mug of coffee and sniffed before taking a sip.

"Mom?"

She put the mug on the counter enthusiastically. "Oh, for God's sake, Marc, of course we didn't. Jesus. We only take it out to Make Out Point."

"Mom!"

"When it comes to sex, my son is a prude."

"I'm a *prude* when my mother is telling my boyfriend about her sex life." He walked over and dropped a kiss on her cheek. "Thank you for coming down, Mother. Please stop talking about sex?"

"One more question," she said, and looked between us. "Condoms?"

"Yes! Of course. Always," Marcus said.

She patted his cheek. "Very good, Marcus. I

approve of this one."

Marcus ran his hand down his face. "Mom... Did you give him the 'don't ghost my son' speech yet?"

"No, because I don't feel like I have to give him the 'don't fuck my son without a condom' speech."

Marcus whirled and stared at me. "Do you have whiskey? I need whiskey. Or stronger. Moonshine? Rubbing alcohol? Sterno?"

I had *no idea* how to handle this. His mother swore, she was open with sex, and she was a total mama bear—don't fuck with her cubs.

I loved her already.

"No, ma'am," I said. "You don't. We're always safe and I have no intention of ghosting your son. I'm afraid I've rather come to like him and I need his support trying to deal with my family."

She waved a hand at me, as if to say, "See?"

Marcus walked to me, dropped a kiss on my lips and headed back to the door. "I'm going to go hide in my apartment and try not to die from embarrassment." The door to the apartment closed, Marcus abandoning me to the whims of his mother.

I glanced at Dawn. "Are you really going to give me a condom speech?"

"No, because I believe you're smart enough to know the speech by heart." She glanced at the door after her son. "When he came out to us, we had to figure out how to raise a gay man. Not that we were going to change the basics like pick up your socks and don't be a jerk to people. But the sex education had to be different." She pinched her nose. "I was terrified.

Terrified, that...

"My older brother was gay, and the hookup culture of today has *nothing* on gay hookup culture of the late 70s and 80s. He was diagnosed with AIDS before it was called that. They were calling it *Kaposi's sarcoma and opportunistic infection* if you felt like being courteous. If not, you called it GRID. In either case, my brother Marcus was diagnosed in 1981, and was dead by '83. I didn't want to see my son suffer that way. We've always kept up on AIDS research and I made sure that not just he, but all of my children were sexually smart."

I traced an 'X' across my chest. "I swear to you, we would never consider it without first having been tested for everything. Because AIDS is not great, and neither is the Clap."

"Good man." She patted my shoulder. "I approve."

I PUSHED open the door of the room, eternally grateful that I had the money for a regular hotel. Maybe the Best Western wasn't the Ritz, but it was better than Betty's Motor Inn in town.

I tossed my bag on the couch. "Welcome to Greenman, Illinois. Middle of Buttfuck Nowhere."

Marcus nodded. "I can see that." He slipped his bag off his shoulder. "It's an interesting...nowhere."

"It's not interesting. It's boring and insular and homophobic and racist. Probably with a good dollop of sexism and misogyny tossed in." I stared out the window of the room. "Christ, I cannot believe I'm back here."

"Would you have left if they hadn't kicked you out?"

"That was the plan. College, anywhere but here, and just never come back." I rubbed my eyes. "I'm not even sure this is the right thing to do. They were horrible to me. I didn't even really have the chance to come out to them. I was outed. I was waiting because I knew they wouldn't want me there anymore. I was going to tell them at a point where I would have been safe."

Marcus slid his arms around my waist and perched his chin on my shoulder. "You don't have to do this."

"You know what stopped me from telling you to turn around and go home? The whole ride here?" He shook his head. "Your mother."

"My mother?"

"She's amazing, Marc. *Fucking* amazing. She just accepts you. She just trusts you. Shit, I'd give my arm to have one sixteenth of the acceptance you have in your family."

"You can borrow her." He laughed.

"Christ, she told us to sleep in the same bed!"

"We're adults."

I turned my head so I could catch his gaze. "She was fine with her son having sex with another man."

"We're gay, that's what it means, right? Enjoying sexual relations with the male of the species? Have I been doing this wrong?" He planted a sloppy kiss on my cheek. "My mom is amazing. I know that. I know she's unique, she'll give hugs to every gay person in the village if they need it. She's accepting, she's open, and she's helped me be the man I am right now." He turned me in his arms to face him. "You can totally borrow her. I'm serious. She'll have you believing you can do anything, love anyone, live anyway you like in about ten seconds. And while I would have loved to have my dad come down, somehow, she knew she was the better option. For *you*."

"Fuck, man," I said, and leaned my forehead on his chest.

"Take everything she gave you in the few hours you chatted and use it. You may never ever get to that point with your parents, but you can take what she said and try."

I nodded against him. "Try. That's why I'm here. They want to try, and I would love it if I could talk to them again. I don't expect this to go well, or to be close to them again, but...just not hating them would be amazing."

"Then let's hope for the best and prepare for the worst."

"The worst being I leave and really truly never come back."

Marcus nodded. "Exactly."

He just stood there holding me, running a hand up and down my back for a minute before I felt him heave a deep breath, and tip his head to look at me. "Did...did my mom really give you the condom talk?"

Laughing, I raised my head. "No, she didn't. She told me about your uncle, though."

"Oh, my namesake." He smiled. "She and her brother were thick as thieves growing up. More than she and Aunt Laura ever were, even though they were closer in age."

"You really are lucky, Marcus. You know that."

"Every day. Every time I meet another member of the community who can't talk to their parents. Every time I see a homeless queer kid on the street. I thank everything in the universe that I have my mom and dad." He kissed me quietly. "And you can borrow them. They really are quite awesome."

I smiled. "I get it. You don't want to be the only one suffering through your mom's condom lecture."

"You see right through me." He laughed.

He danced us backward to the bed, and before I knew what was going on, he had me down on the mattress, and he stood over me. I lifted up on my elbows and studied him.

"You look good enough to eat, Chase." His hand reached for my belt. "In fact, I think I will."

His hand flicked open the buckle, and all I could do was nod and make incomprehensible noises. He had me out of the pants and out of my boxers in record time and before I could say a thing, he slipped his lips over the crown of my half hard...*nope*, fully hard dick.

My mind blanked. The only thing I liked more than Marcus' mouth on me, was his cock *in* me. Or was it my cock in him? At that moment, I didn't care. His tongue licked around me, and then up the insanely sensitive underside, and then across my slit.

I didn't know how many times we'd done this, either him to me or me to him. It didn't matter. Each and every time was as good or better than the last.

He swallowed me down to the root—which was a

totally new trick for him and made me squeal. "Holy shit, Marcus!"

Bobbing his head up and down a few times, he stopped and waited for me to look at him. He pulled off me completely, and grinned. "Watch me, Chase. I want you to watch me suck you."

I was totally unsure if anything even remotely like English came out of my mouth. It was more *buhblergarghohshhhh,* but it worked. Marcus kept going, and he loved that I watched him. It was his usual request. I could feel the head of my dick bumping the back of his throat, and his throat closing around me in a ripple. It was a mind-blowing sensation.

Cock blowing? Whatever.

He swallowed at the same time he caressed the under side with that tongue of his. He moved, bobbing up and down on my erection, swallowing and licking, twisting a bit.

His hand found my balls and cradled them a moment. Shit, his fingers felt good. He was firm and gentle, massaging them while he still speared me into his throat. All the while, he would not let my eyes go. He watched me watching him.

"Oh, God, Marcus..."

He pulled off completely. "You gonna come for me, baby? I want you in my mouth."

I nodded as he dropped back down. "I'm going to come. Just keep going, babe. Suck me down. Had no idea you could deep throat me—*ahhhh!*"

The pad of his thumb brushed over my hole, stopping and pressing there, teasing me. It wasn't expected, and I came hard without warning.

Marcus swallowed every drop of my cum. I could see the mirth in his eyes after the lust tampered down a moment after my last thrust. He licked and sucked his way back up my cock, and let it pop out with a lascivious sound, echoing in the room.

"Someone liked that." He grinned, and wiped his chin with the back of his hand.

Even that was sexy.

"I'll let you know when something you do doesn't feel good or make me come in seconds."

He stood and crawled up the bed. "What if it's something you don't like *and* it makes you come in seconds?"

"I somehow think that's not possible," I was still blissed out and flopped back, staring at the ceiling, but I managed to find Marcus' buckle and free him from his pants one handed. I lazily stroked his rock hard erection.

"Mmm," he breathed. "That feels good. Just...keep doing that."

He was happy with my lazy hand job, for a few minutes. But eventually, he had better ideas for his cock. And I was all for it.

CHAPTER EIGHTEEN

MARCUS

THE GARCIA FARM WAS A WORK IN progress. The farmhouse in the center of the land was old. Really old, but it had an addition on the back and was well taken care of. The barn was restored and it looked like there was a ring for horseback riding. There was another smaller barn, way more modern, that seemed to hold the equipment.

And way in the back was a small house, with a dirt path leading to a porch that was just teeming with flower pots and trays.

It was clear that the Garcias were no longer farmers, save for some token acreage around the house. There was corn, as seemed to be required in Illinois, as well as soybeans, wheat, and a giant patch of vines.

"Pumpkin?" I asked.

Chase smiled at the vines on the right. "It was my

Abuelita's idea, after Abuelo died. She wanted to do something fun with the farm, not make my dad and mom farm for a living, but not give it up completely. The Garcia Pumpkin Patch is one of the county's best. Dad rotated it through the fields each year."

He pointed to the distance where there was more corn and soybean fields, that were more typical of farms. "That's still our land, but dad leased it to a collective and lets them plant and harvest what they need to." Pausing, he glanced out to the corn. "Their land. Not mine. Not ours. Theirs."

I didn't react to his words. "So you grew up with a pumpkin patch?"

"Oh, yeah." Chase smiled, looking back. "I loved working the pumpkins in October. It was so much fun. Abuelita and I would go out in the middle of September and start weeding and moving the pumpkins into rows. It was a lot of work, but she and I would walk and move and sing some of the songs she remembered from when she was little in Spain."

"So you're Spanish?"

"Half Spanish, half Latino. Mom's family came up from Mexico in the early 1800s. One of my greats hated the heat and moved the whole family up here. Cortez, no relation."

I laughed. "I didn't think so."

"My grandmother and grandfather's family fled Spain in the 30s, just before Franco took over. They were so young. Abeulita was just five."

"Do you speak Spanish?"

"Only my grandmother's Galician, which is long

mangled and sounds more like Portuguese than anything else." He laughed.

"Is the little old lady watering the flowers on that porch your grandmother?"

He spun and looked. A smile like no other I had seen lit up his face, and he popped the door open. He jumped out, and ran for the little dirt path. I shut the car off and climbed out, following at a more reasonable pace.

"Abuelita!" he screamed like a twelve year old.

She jerked her head up and I could see the shock on her face as we headed closer. She dropped her watering can and came around the pillars and down the stairs. "Chase?"

He slowed just enough to not knock the woman off her feet and instead wrap her in a huge hug. He could clearly have lifted the woman off the ground in his joy, and that said something because she was not a tiny person. She was maybe two inches shorter than Chase.

I listened as I walked closer and slowed about ten feet away from them.

"Oh, *dios mio*, Chase. Where the hell have you been? Child, I have been worried sick about you!"

"They never told you?" he asked, still hugging her.

"No! They said you left and that was it. No one said anything about you after that." She held him away from her, and studied him, pushing his hair out of his face. "Ay, child, you're grown."

"I've been living in New York," he said. "I can't believe they didn't tell you anything."

"My son is a stubborn ass," she said. She studied him. "Did they tell you..."

"Rider came to get me, and hoped I wouldn't come."

She threw her head back and laughed. "And so you did. That's the Chase I know." She glanced over at me. "And who is that?"

I had to bite my lip. She was eyeballing me like other people eyeballed a prime cut of meat. Chase shook his head, but I saw him take a deep breath at the same time. "Abuelita, this is Marcus. My boyfriend."

"Mmm," was all she said. She stepped back from Chase and circled me like she was sizing up some livestock for sale. I bit my lip again, and choked on the laugh.

Her eyes slipped over to Chase, and he sighed. She walked over to him, took his hand and gave him an enormous grin. "Nicely done, Grandson. This gentleman is a fine specimen."

"Wait...what..." The confusion on his face was comical.

She shook her finger at him. "Your parents and your brother's prejudices are the tiny thoughts of tiny minds in this tiny town. I didn't live here growing up. I grew up in a huge colony of Spaniards who fled from Franco's rule. Artists, musicians, artisans. A man and man having an affair? Feh! Nothing! My uncle—he was married to a woman, yes, but they shared a lover, a man. Who even knows if my cousin Maria Alina is actually my blood cousin? Doesn't matter. Hildago made them happy."

Chase and I stared at each other. His great uncle had been in a poly relationship? Holy crap.

"So, you and this handsome man? Whatever. As long as you care about each other and have fun. In bed, out of bed, doesn't matter."

Turning bright red, Chase ran a hand over his face. "Abuelita…"

"Would you like to come in for some coffee before you walk into Hell?" she asked sweetly.

"Abuelita… Hell?"

She looked around the two of us to the driveway. "Ah, Rider isn't here. Perhaps you should go talk to them now. Rider hasn't exactly been the most supportive of your father trying to talk to you."

"Mom sent him to find me?"

"Your father." She nodded. She leaned in. "I had to explain Hildago to him as well before he got it. I didn't enjoy explaining what a three-way was to my own son."

Chase pinched the bridge of his nose, and I just did what I could to keep from busting out laughing. "What do you think? Is it smarter for me to go in without Rider?"

"I do," she said. "Leave the boy toy here with me. I'll feed him and water him, and when you're ready for him to come join you or rescue you, I'll send him over."

Shaking his head, it was clear Chase wasn't going to be happy with that. "No. I want him with me. I am not going in there alone. I can't, Abuelita. I got kicked out of there on my ass, and I'm not sure coming back was the right thing to do..."

"Phone?" She held her hand out.

Chase held it out, and she took it from him. Like anyone who was used to handling a cell, she had her contact information in there in a flash. She motioned for mine next and inputted the contact there. Handing it back, I took a quick look at the screen. *Maria Felicia (Abuelita)* was typed in there—at least now I knew her name.

"You have one hour to text me, Chase. Or I'm texting your man to tell me to come drag you out." She dropped a kiss on his cheek. "And then you're going to come over and we can have dinner and catch up."

"Don't worry, Abuelita. I'm not letting your contact in my phone get cold." He laughed.

"*Bueno.*" She nodded. "Go. Deal with my idiot son and his wife." She rolled her eyes to the sky and shook her head.

He took my hand and we headed back toward the car.

"The female of the species is in mourning for the loss of you, Marcus!"

"Oh, my God, I forgot about her sass mouth," Chase groaned.

"I'd say the same to you, Chase, but I'm your grandmother and that's gross!"

I burst out laughing, finally. "Holy crap, Chase, she's amazing!"

"Right? I didn't have a chance to tell her anything before they ran me out of town." He sighed. "I've missed her so much, but I was scared she was on their side. I couldn't bear it if my grandmother rejected me because I was gay. I just didn't talk to her."

"She wants to make up for it."

"Marcus, she's nuts." He smirked. "I love her so much."

"Good, we'll have dinner there. It's gotta be better than Spacey Jo's Buttermilk Hell."

He laughed. "I can't believe that place was still there. And just as bad as I remember. I'm dying for some real food. They still fry and sauce everything here."

"They do." I nodded. "I never thought I'd say this, but I'd kill for some kale."

The laughter wasn't there this time. His manner was becoming more subdued as we reached the car, and a moment later he was leaning on the trunk. Chase wrapped his arms around himself, and looked at me.

"Is this the right thing to do?"

"Yes," I answered. I wasn't sure, really, but it was what he needed to hear. "Just the chance to wrap this up one way or another with them. Finish this chapter in the book."

He took back the hand he had released a moment before. "You'll be there. But Marcus...let me talk. Don't jump to my defense, don't try to intercede. I *need* to have this closure. Rider was different, because he insulted you, but these are my parents...and I..."

I squeezed his hand. "I get it, babe. I am there for you to lean on, figuratively and literally, if you need it.

But I am going to be listening for your grandmother's text."

Nodding, and not letting go of my hand this time, we headed for the front door of the house. When we were on the porch, I let go of him and stood back, against the porch support, a good ten feet from the door. Chase saw what I was doing and I could tell he wanted me closer. It wasn't smart though.

I wasn't about to shove our relationship in their face.

Chase lifted his hand and knocked on the door. Three hard, short raps, and stepped back just a little. We waited. It was a good minute before I heard the tumblers in the door turn to open.

The door swung in, and the mirror image of Chase stood on the other side—save with white hair and sallow skin. Right down to the blue eyes. And each set of them was frozen on the other.

Chase cleared his throat. "Hi, Dad."

The man blinked a few times, wrinkled his brow, then finally cleared his throat. "Chase?"

"Yeah," he answered. "It's me."

"So, then, Rider found you."

"You always knew where I was," he answered.

"You didn't call."

Chase huffed. "You didn't either."

The older man pursed his lips. "I'm doing this wrong, Chase." His son looked like he was about to lay into him, but held up a hand to stave him off. "I don't want to fight. I'm done fighting with people." He moved his hand from its raised position into an offer to shake. "Thank you for coming, Son."

Slowly, Chase reached his hand out and shook his father's hand. "You could have picked someone better than Rider to ask me."

"You're telling me? He hasn't shut up about the cocksucker comment since he came home." His father tossed a look at me standing there. "Well done, young man. Not much throws Rider out of his own orbit. He needed it."

I nodded in acknowledgement.

He turned back to Chase. "Come in, please, Son. Bring your friend in. Too damn hot out here for me."

Chase tossed a look at me, and I moved up so I could follow him into the house. We walked into the foyer and the cool of the air conditioning washed over us while I closed the door behind me. I could see where the back of the house had the addition, and the stairs were straight up on the left. There was a bench, and a small table with flowers, and whitewashed wainscoting ran along the walls.

"Tony? Who is it?"

A woman just a little shorter than Chase and his dad appeared in the door to the kitchen. She was wearing a sunny yellow apron, skinny jeans and striped top. Her hair, a more muted gray and black, was up in a messy bun.

She gasped and put a hand to her mouth, staring at Chase. "Is that really you?"

"Hi, Mom."

She launched herself at him, and the tears just burst out of her. "Oh, my God, Chase. Chase, I'm so sorry! I'm so sorry. I didn't know what to do or how to talk to you or—"

"Don't smother the damn kid, Beth," Tony grumbled. "Get him back and kill him with kindness. Damn."

The small chuckle escaped me, and I covered my mouth with the back of my hand. Chase extracted himself from his mother and took my hand. "Mom, Dad, this is my boyfriend, Marcus. Marcus, these are my parents, Tony and Beth Garcia."

I reached out and shook each of their hands. "Nice to meet you."

Tony shook his head. "Doesn't just come back, has to bring a boyfriend. Lord. Come on, come into the kitchen. I got some beers and we can chat."

Beth looked terrified for just a moment. "Tony, I'm not—"

"Beth, the boy doesn't care if your stove has stains. He doesn't. Just come in and sit with him. Damn."

This was going to be interesting.

CHAPTER NINETEEN

CHASE

THE KITCHEN WAS STILL YELLOW.

I'd bet the living room was still blue, the dining room still gray, and their bedroom still beige. My room would still have the boats and sails from when I was ten, and Rider's room was probably still full of race cars.

Things didn't change on the Garcia farm.

Well, maybe that wasn't so true anymore.

My grandmother living in the old cottage was one of the changes. I hoped there were going to be more.

My father took a drink of the beer. I was going to make a comment about the 11:30 in the morning beer, but I didn't think it would be the best move.

"So, uh…" He spun the can of cheap brew in his hands, and stared at it. It took him a minute to look up again. "I owe you an apology. Whether or not I agreed with your lifestyle, I was wrong to throw you out and I was wrong to not listen to you. I'm sorry for that."

I just about fell off my chair. It wasn't the most elegant apology, and certainly not the purest, but it was an apology.

"Thank you, Dad," I managed.

"This *How to Die* therapy they have me in—"

"It's not *How to Die*," my mother snapped.

"Oh, jeeze, this again..." He shook his head. "Fine. The Death With Dignity therapy I'm in has me talking about what I screwed up in life..."

My mother let out a giant sigh. "It's a Death With Dignity therapy designed to help end-of-life patients deal with their own grief, and the regrets they might have. It also encourages different thinking and both trying to rectify regrets and living with them."

Dad was staring at the ceiling until Mom was done. "So. That thing. And it did get me thinking—"

"After he finished cursing me out and being an ass about all of this," my mother added.

"—that I don't have a whole lot of time left. Maybe these head shrinkers weren't completely wrong about things."

I held up my hand. "Hold on. I have *no idea* what's going on here. Someone has to tell me why Rider showed up at my house telling me you were dying in six months, and I had to come out here."

"I have primary amyloidosis, I have for a few *years*," Dad said. "We've been able to control it pretty well, but in the past six months the drugs I need to control it have needed to be upped, and my body isn't responding very well anymore. I'm going into congestive left heart failure."

"The doctor said there are more treatments—" Mom started.

"Beth. We've been through this. I don't want the treatments. I don't want to be put on a transplant list. I'm not taking a healthy heart away from a twenty year old. I'm sixty-five and I've lived my life. Let a kid have it."

"So," I interrupted again, "you're dying but it's not like, you're going to keel over tomorrow."

"They're going to put in a pacemaker next week," Dad said. "But there's not much they can do for the muscle actually toughening up. With the pacemaker they're thinking two to four years. But I could have a cardiac incident that did me in, in a month, six months, a year from now. My heart just isn't up to snuff anymore."

There were tears in my mother's eyes—Antonio Garcia was her life, and to hear him talking like this had to be breaking her own heart.

"All right, so why didn't Mom just say something on the phone to me."

"I told her not to," Dad answered. "I did you wrong, Son. I treated you poorly. I asked Rider to talk to you, but apparently he decided going to the city would be more effective. When I found out he went, I was hoping that maybe, just maybe, he'd see what I've been really learning all this time between the therapy and Reverend Gil."

Oh, God. Here it went. Reverend Gil was going to be a pseudo-ally who kept telling everyone to love the sinner, hate the sin. Or some other such bullshit-fueled platitude that allowed you to keep preaching at

The Gays while still pretending you cared.

"Your father and I changed churches about a year ago," Mom said.

That caught me off guard. The Garcias and the Cortezes had gone to Paris Lutheran for...generations. "What? Are you serious?"

Mom nodded. "Pastor Allen was a nice man, but we both felt that his utter hatred of non-Lutherans was getting a bit much. I...*we* were having trouble sitting in the pews listening to him tell us that there was no redemption for our son. That he was going to Hell because he *layeth with another man*."

"Meanwhile," Dad continued. "Victor Darren's wife Marilyn was raped and murdered about that time."

I gasped, "Mrs. Darren? Sweet Mrs. Darren who taught second grade at the school?"

Dad nodded solemnly. "Well, they caught the guy, and it turned out it was one of Pastor Allen's friend's kids. He stood up there with that murdering bastard child, and told the court he was a good man, a man of God, who had made a mistake. Andy—who was deputy sheriff and one of the first on the scene—heard that, he got up and left the courtroom. He told me later it was no *mistake* when the victim had been stabbed fifty-seven times. And that wasn't counting the brutal rape, which he would never tell me more about, save to say it was savage."

Mom picked up the story. "So, there's Pastor Allen preaching forgiveness for this man who destroyed a family, a school and a community, but on Sunday he was in that pulpit telling us how our law abiding, non-rapist son who happens to prefer men to women was going to Hell."

Dad cleared his throat. "Now, Reverend Gil is a good man. He doesn't like to just tell us how to think. He doesn't like that. He wants all of his sheep to think for themselves and not just follow the flock. When I sat down with him, on recommendation of my therapist—"

Who was this man? Talking to therapists? Spiritual counselors?

"—he brought out a Bible, like he knew exactly what I was thinking about with all this *how to die* therapy."

My mother huffed and rolled her eyes.

Dad spun the can of beer in his hands a few times. Even in the air conditioning of the house, the aluminum was sweating, and he seemed to chase the droplet around it.

"Reverend Gil open the Bible, and showed me all the places where it was the Lord had said thou shall not kill. There were hundreds. New and old testament. Some were like the Commandments, 'Thou shalt not kill,' and others were more poetic. But they all followed that same Commandment.

"Then, he pointed out all the parts of the same book where it says 'Thou shalt not lie with a man as you would with a woman,' in whatever flowy poetry you wanted to frame it.

"There are seven. Just seven. And four of those are up for serious debate." He played with the tab on the beer can. "Reverend said that homosexuality is a modern concept. That as psychology began to understand that gender was a construct, they needed words for it. And he said that in the past fifty, Hell, twenty years, the understanding of sex, sexuality, and gender has exploded and expanded and the...Kinsey scale? is an oversimplification of a very complex concept."

My mother leaned forward. "And then the Reverend Gil introduced us to his boyfriend."

I saw Marcus sit back in his chair in shock and I was right there with him. That was not the way I had expected that to go at all. Not at all.

"Nice man," Dad said. "One of the boys from the dairy farm up the road. Hard worker, strong faith. Was a little weird to see them making googly eyes at each other, but..." He took a deep breath and looked straight at me. "Who am I to judge. If they make each other happy, isn't that really all we can ask out of this life?"

Fuck. Me. He apologized. In his own Antonio Garcia way, he apologized to me.

I stood from my chair, and walked around to him. Leaning down, I wrapped my arms around him and hugged him. Hard. As hard as I could.

He sniffled. I knew he was crying. "Wish I'd realized that with more time on the clock but—"

"We still *have* time on the clock, Dad."

My mother let out a huge sob, and covered her mouth trying not to ugly cry. Marcus was seated with his arms folded and a smile on his face.

ABUELITA WALKED up the steps of the front porch where my father and I sat on the porch swing. She was carrying a basket of something.

"Momma, why didn't you call and have one of us come over?" Dad said.

"Because you've got less time on your ticker than I do, Antonio. So shut your yap and let me bring over my fried chicken."

"Oh, shit, Abuelita, are you serious?" I gasped, just as the smell hit my nose. "You are!"

"Do I smell fried chicken?" Marcus called from behind her, walking up with our bags. "Oh, God, Maria, tell me that's really homemade fried chicken?"

"I put it in the buttermilk this morning."

"Praise Jeebus," he mumbled.

I pulled the door open for the two of them, and watched as my grandmother made her way to the back of the house. I held up a finger to have Marcus wait, and I smiled.

"Oh, Momma! Yes!" my mother yelled from the kitchen.

"No one makes fried chicken like Abuelita." I smiled.

Marcus laughed, dropping a quick peck on my lips and headed inside. My parents had insisted we stay with them through the weekend, and when I had seen they hadn't left my room with the single bed and sailboats and had instead painted it neutral and put a queen in it—I realized they really were trying. Maybe more than trying.

"Who do you have taking care of the pumpkins?"

"Rider is supposed to, but he's not exactly good at it. Momma has some neighbor boys she pays. She loves that patch. And honestly, so do I and your mother. It's not just income. It's a tradition."

"Does it bother you that you can't work it?"

"Some days. Other days, I'm glad for the porch and a cold beer and the chance to just sit." He sighed. "How's your shoulder?"

"Oh, long healed," I answered. "I got to a clinic and had them help me out. Took a lot of the money I had saved, but I got it straight."

"Are you set there in New York?"

"Great apartment, great coworkers, two cats, one dog, and a boyfriend." I smiled. "That's about as good as it gets."

"He treats you right?"

I nodded. "Yeah. He does."

"Good." He patted my knee.

"The prodigal son returns."

We both turned and found Rider mounting the steps to the side of the porch. He had a scowl on his face, and he was filthy from whatever he was doing.

"I came to make peace with my father, Rider. I have no beef with you."

"Did you let Mom slaughter the fatted calf?"

"Rider..." My father shook his head.

"I'm not here to fight."

"Of course not! Everything is fine now, isn't it? We're all happy with the fag in the family!"

I had no idea where Marcus had come from, but he slugged Rider right in the jaw and sent him stumbling sideways into the railing.

Marcus dropped his fists to his side and stared my brother down. "I'm not just good at cocksucking, jackass. I'm also pretty good at sucker punches."

"What is wrong with you people?" Rider screamed at our father. "Why the hell are you suddenly okay with queers? Why don't you see how disgusting this is? How unnatural!"

"That's your problem now, Son," Dad said, calmly. "You keep saying those words and thinking those thoughts, and people like Marcus here, are going to keep educating you on what *equal rights* and *shut your damn mouth* mean." He jerked his head at the door. "Go inside. Abuelita and your mother will get you some ice for that jaw. Marcus, I'll say this just once. Don't hit my son, no matter how much he needs it."

"Yes, sir. Sorry."

"Apologies go to the offended."

I had to hold back the snort that threatened me. My dad was still my dad. But Marcus nodded and walked into the house. I saw my dad's eyebrows shoot up when the door closed.

"He just went in there to apologize?"

"Yes. Marcus is an amazing man, Dad." I ran a hand over my mouth and leaned against the railing and looked at the door where he had disappeared. "I don't know if it's the right way for things to happen, but I am seriously, seriously falling hard for him."

"Son, Chase...there is no right or wrong when it comes to falling in love. There are no timelines." He let out a sigh. "I love your mom with all my heart, and we've been fighting about this heart thing for months. Of *fucking* course I want more time with her. A thousand years wouldn't be enough with her. We fight, but half the fun of it is making up."

"Dad..."

"Sorry not sorry," he said, waving me off. "What I'm trying to say is that if you think you're in love with him, don't waste time."

"Sage advice from an old man."

"Not that old."

"Then why aren't you on the transplant list?"

He shook his head. "She wants me on the transplant list, but I'm not young. Where do I get off taking a heart from an eighteen or twenty year old who hasn't had a chance to live?"

"I get the selfless act, Dad, I do. But if you're otherwise healthy, why shouldn't you get a chance at another twenty years?"

"Because those kids could get sixty or eighty out of it."

I ran a hand down my face. "Will you let me do some research? Be open to other ideas?"

"Of course." He nodded. "If you can work on immortality for me and your mother, that would be great."

Marcus pushed back out of the house, red and shaking and hurried down the stairs around the house with a quiet "excuse me."

My father tossed his chin at him. "Go. See what Rider did this time."

I trotted after Marcus, hopping down the stairs, hoping he wasn't too far ahead of me. I only made it just around the corner before he grabbed me and shoved me against the house. His mouth was crashing over mine, and I groaned quietly against his lips.

The kiss lasted a while, going back and forth from

hard and soft, and finally he pulled away, resting his forehead on mine. "Sorry. I just needed a reminder why I put up with homophobes."

I groaned, "You stopped..."

He laughed. "You want more, baby?"

"Yes," I whined.

I watched his lips curl in a smile. "Why don't we go find out if hay is actually worth rolling in?"

I grabbed his hand and ran.

Hay was totally worth rolling in.

☆

MARCUS

I PICKED another piece of hay out of my hair and shook my head. I'd forgotten that hay got *everywhere,* and it was sticky. Not gooey-sticky, but thorny-sticky.

Chase's hand trailed up and down my back, trying to distract me or entice me, who knew.

I sighed and turned to him. I whispered at him, "Sweetheart, I told you when we agreed to stay here, I'm not fucking you in your parents' house, in your childhood bedroom."

"Hayloft is fine," he said.

Leaning down, I kissed his nose. "I'm going to look like the hayloft if we keep that up."

"Mmm, my own personal sexy scarecrow."

"No. Never say that again." But I was laughing. "Meanwhile, I smell breakfast."

He flopped back in the bed. "I think I'm still full from Abuelita's chicken last night."

"Or are you still full from our second trip to the barn?"

He shook a lazy finger at me. "Do not pervert the fried chicken." His hand dropped to the bed. "Damn you, Marcus. Now I'm hard."

It had been mostly the memory of our second trip to the barn than anything else. He'd said fast and dirty, and I obliged. I was sure his ass still twinged.

"Now? You've been hard since you woke up twenty minutes ago."

"Have pity on me, baby!" he cried, poking my side with his finger.

In the next instant, he was biting his fist in his mouth because in one smooth motion, I had turned, pulled the sheets down and swallowed his cock whole.

He was not ready.

After a few bobs and licks, I pulled off and gave him a devilish grin. "You want it, you got it. No noise, sweetheart, or I'm going to have to spank you."

"That's not a threa—ah!"

Honestly, I'd had no intention of giving him a blow job because this was his childhood bedroom in his parents' house and that was just weird. But as soon as he said he was hard, I couldn't ignore the lust anymore.

It was fun to try and make him scream or groan than to make him come, so I kept edging my poor boyfriend. He squirmed and made muffled sounds— he bit his lips and fist—he cover his eyes with his arm and tried not to even whimper.

Chase tasted delicious. I would never ever tire of tasting him, his cock, his balls, his cum. His skin was flushed and warm and the muscles of his thighs rippled as he squirmed. His nipples were pearled and his expression was one of bliss.

But even more, I liked being around him. He was sweet, strong, handsome...willing to forgive. He had come to see his father despite the fear of a second rejection.

I couldn't help myself with this man.

Slipping a finger over the sensitive skin around his hole, I petted him lightly while sucking hard and finally allowed him to fall over the edge into the bliss of orgasm.

"Shit!" he yelled.

I won.

I grinned around his dick, taking every drop of cum he wanted to offer me. He whimpered as I drank him down, and cleaned him off, very thoroughly. So thoroughly, he was starting to get hard again.

"Oh, God, no more right now. My cock is willing but the flesh is spongy and bruised."

My laugh erupted out of me. "Did you just quote Zapf Brannigan?"

"What of it? He was right."

Flopping down on my stomach next to him, I kissed his cheek. "God, I love you."

Whoa.

There was a terrible banging on the door downstairs. We jerked and looked toward the hall. Without another word, we quickly pulled on some clothes and made our way down the stairs.

Beth was hurrying from the kitchen to the door. She pulled it open.

There was a tall, built man standing there, holding his hat, while two more men—currently nothing more than two pair of shoes and a shadow—stood behind him.

"Del Billings, what are you doing here?" Beth's smile was wide.

"Mrs. Garcia. I'm afraid we're not here to make a social call. May we come in?"

"Of course..." She was as confused as we were, but stepped out of the way.

The three of them walked into the foyer, and the sheriff's eyes shot to me and Chase on the stairs. "Mister Romano?"

I nodded.

He held up a blue-backed piece of paper, and my legs went out from under me, landing me hard on my ass on the stairs.

I had seen too many of those pieces of paper in my life.

"Marcus?" Chase's voice sounded miles away from me, and it slogged through the buzzing in my head. "Marcus!" His hand slid into mine and his palm was against my cheek.

Glancing back at the sheriff I could see the remorse in his eyes as he handed the paper over to Tony to inspect, then turned back to me. "Mister Romano, we have a warrant for your arrest from the State of New York, Kings County, with an extradition agreement for the State of Illinois."

"W-what—" I choked on the words. I didn't want to know.

"What charges?" Chase asked.

"As stated by the District Attorney in Kings County," the sheriff said, "Rape in the First Degree,

Criminal Sexual Act in the First Degree, and
Predatory Sexual Assault."

I managed to stumble up the steps into the
bathroom and heaved everything out of my stomach
at once. I was choking on my own vomit when Chase
slammed to his knees next to me and ran a careful
hand over my back.

"Breathe, Marcus, please."

My head hung low, and the world spun and
twisted around. I couldn't believe this was happening
again.

Beth reached over me and flushed, and a moment
later she was holding out a paper cup of mouthwash.
"Rinse, Marcus. It will help you get your bearings."

I obeyed, swishing, and spitting back into the
bowl.

"Do you have a lawyer in New York?" she asked.

"N-no," I managed between horrid and ragged
breaths.

"You will by the time you get there," Chase said.

"Call my mom, please," I managed. "Please."

"I will," Beth said.

Barely managing to get my feet under me, I stood
and walked to the door. Chase and Beth had me by the
arms, and helped me down the stairs. The sheriff was
at the bottom and he was holding out handcuffs.

"*No!*" I gasped, backing up. "Please, no, sir. No. I
will come with you without trouble. Please don't put
those on me."

He must have seen how I was trembling, and
nodded, hooking them back on his belt.

Chase grabbed the warrant. "Do you need this

back?"

"'Fraid so," he said.

"Can you wait just two minutes while I make a copy for his lawyer?"

I sobbed, "Chase, I don't—"

He leaned up and kissed me. "You totally have a lawyer. Don't say anything to anyone, babe. Not one word. Got it?"

Nodding, I watched him sprint into the office at the back of the house, and came back less than a minute later with his copy and the original.

The sheriff took my elbow and led me down the stairs.

I was reliving my worst fucking nightmare, and I didn't know how to wake up.

CHAPTER TWENTY

CHASE

THE PATROL CAR HADN'T EVEN TURNED around with Marcus in the back before I had the phone to my ear. I knew exactly who to call.

"Vincent Bartrand."

"Vin, it's Chase. I need to put you on professional retainer, right now, and for you to meet my boyfriend at central booking when they get there."

"Excuse me? Your boyfriend? Aren't you in Illinois?"

"Yes, I am. At my parents' place. The sheriff just carted away Marcus on an arrest warrant for New York." I knew I was talking fast even for New York, but Vincent was a lawyer and if he couldn't keep up, he needed to quit. "I have a copy of the arrest warrant here. Do you want me to send it to you? I already told him not to talk to anyone. I'm going to pack my shit in a few minutes and get on the road home, but I need—"

"Stop," Vincent's voice snapped down the line. "Take a goddamn breath."

I did, and I was shocked that I was panting from my tirade. My hands were shaking, and my mother grabbed the copies of the warrant out of my hand so I didn't crush or destroy them in any other way.

"Okay. Your boyfriend is being extradited to Kings County for what?"

"Rape charges."

There was silence. It was too long of a silence, and I finally called through the phone. "Still there, Vincent?"

"I am...you know I don't handle..."

"Fuck," I snapped at him. "He didn't rape anyone! He didn't hurt anyone! He ripped open the wall of my living room to rescue kittens! He's not a rapist."

"Okay, all right, calm down. I'll call someone to help me. He's not cheap..."

"I don't care about money. Get my boyfriend out of jail and these charges dropped. Vincent, please, for me."

"Yes, of course," he said. "Email the copies you have and I'll get on it. How long until you're back?"

"It's a thirteen hour drive, so if I get going now, I'll have to crash overnight. Even if I could walk out the door right now I won't be there before noon tomorrow."

"Crash somewhere, man," Vincent said. "Do not go thirteen hours yourself. We've got it on this end.

Isn't his mother here?"

"Yes," I said.

"Good. Call her and she'll be ready for him and me."

"Thank you, Vin. Seriously."

"Chase, I'm not kidding about that bill from this guy."

"And I'm not kidding about not giving a shit," I answered.

"All right. I'll see you tomorrow, mid-afternoon."

"Done."

We closed the connections and I looked at my mother and father standing there.

My father cleared his throat. "Chase—"

"He didn't rape anyone," I snapped.

"That isn't what I was going to say," Dad answered. "I was going to ask if you wanted to get a plane ticket and we'd get the car back to you."

"Oh." I blinked a few times. "Thank you. It's not even Marcus' car. It's his mother's and I think I should probably drive it back."

Mom pulled her apron off and tossed it on the railing as she walked up the stairs. "Come on. Let's get everything packed and get you back on the road. He's going to need your help."

Between the two of us, we managed to get my stuff and his bag packed in under half an hour. I hauled them out to the car, and dropped them into the backseat and trotted into the house.

Abuelita was sitting at the table with my father,

and they were both drinking coffee quietly. They looked up and my father nodded at me. "Would you like anyone to go with you, Son?"

"No, Dad, you all stay. I'll have Dawn there to help me. If I need back up I'll call."

"You'll call anyway?" Abuelita asked.

"I will come back for the pumpkins if I can." I smiled. Now that shit had cleared up here with them, I wanted to bring Marcus back and show him the glory of the Garcia Pumpkin Patch in October.

But I needed to get back to the city. Giving Abuelita and my dad a quick kiss and hug in that order, I headed to the front door to get in the car and get going.

My mother walked with me to the door and out onto the porch, just to find Rider walking up with his wife behind him. He looked surprised I was heading out the door, but I took a hard right to go down the second set of stairs to the left of the house.

"Where's your butt buddy?" Rider laughed.

"Rider, please," Mom begged. "Your brother doesn't need that right now. He just wants to leave."

"I am leaving," I said, stepping on to the first stair.

"Ooh, did they arrest him already?"

I froze.

"Rider, what have you done?" Mom whispered.

"I was at the station and I saw the fugitive warrant come up." He shrugged. "When I saw the name and suspected location, I brought it over to Chief Prader. He sent the information to the sheriff."

I turned slowly and stepped back up on to the porch.

"You did what?"

"Just being a good citizen," he smirked. "Fugitive warrants are no joke. I mean, what did you really expect from a freak of nature? All homosexuals are perverts and just grooming kids to be the same kind of sick they are."

I didn't have a chance to punch him in the face. My mother walked up to him and I was *sure* her smack across his face dislocated his jaw.

Rider's mouth hung open, staring at her. He tried to say something, anything, and just as he got his voice back, she smack him again. Harder.

"Get off my porch."

I had never, ever heard that tone in my mother's voice before. It was terrifying.

"Mom, I—"

"I said, *get off my fucking porch*!"

Dad and Abuelita were in the door by now. Even they stepped back when those words flew out of her mouth. Hell, Rider took a step back.

"I just got my son back after twelve years of that exact goddamn attitude! He's gay, Rider! He's not a murderer, he's not a pedophile. He's gay! He happens to like other men instead of women. Marcus had no intention of coming onto you! He had no intention of touching you or making a pass or actually sucking your—" She cut herself off. "Now, instead of dealing with this in New York, where he might have been able to avoid an arrest, you've brought the law down on his head. You've managed to get my son's boyfriend arrested. I hope to *God* they can clear that!"

She stared at him, and then looked over at his wife and then back to him.

I didn't even know my brother's wife's name.

"He's an abomination before God," Rider said the words, but the conviction was wavering.

"Get off my porch," Elizabeth Maria Cortez Garcia growled at her son. "And don't show your face here again until you realize that someone who loves someone is never a sinner! *Go!*"

Rider turned, jumped, and ran from the porch. He jumped into the car and a minute later, peeled down the driveway.

The woman who was my brother's wife hung her head and I saw tears in her eyes. So did Abuelita, who rushed over to her and wrapped her in her arms. "Rachel, sweetie..."

She looked up. "We were coming to tell you...I'm pregnant and we're getting a divorce."

My mother and father gasped, and I think my grandmother and I did as well.

"Oh, sweetheart, I'm so sorry," Abuelita said, hugging her tight.

"I don't want to cut you out of the baby's life..."

My mother held up a finger. "Chase, go help your man. I'll talk to you about Rachel and Rider later. You need to get on the road, now."

Nodding, I gave her and my grandmother a quick

peck on the cheek. Dad got a hug, and Rachel, my now soon to be ex-sister-in-law, got a sympathetic shoulder squeeze. I ran off the porch, and slid in to the car.

I promised myself that Marcus and I would be back for the Pumpkin Patch, and drove away from the farm, not for the last time.

CHAPTER TWENTY-ONE

MARCUS

I REALLY HATED HANDCUFFS.

The sheriff had been nice enough to understand and trust me not to do anything. Since I wasn't planning anything, that was agreeable.

The detective that came to get me from the city was a different story all together. For some reason he wanted me in chains. Hands and ankles. It was only when I puked on his new shoes that he got the idea he was either going to keep me out of them, or he was going to have to figure out how to move a very heavy, very unconscious human.

We flew back from Cincinnati. He insisted on the cuffs the whole way. I tried to explain I wasn't going to run because I wasn't guilty. I didn't want to incriminate myself by trying to get away from him. And on a plane? What was I going to do? Unplug the smoke detector in the bathroom?

Once we landed at JFK, there were two uniformed officers there to take me to central booking, and central booking in a city like New York was its own experience. Loud, crowded, people were milling around everywhere. This was where the criminals of the petty and grand sort met and had pissing contests.

I sat quietly in a holding cell.

I couldn't believe I was here again.

I thought I had left all this bullshit behind. I had barely made it out of the Conservatory with my degree, last time. I had no reputation, and the few friends I had left had hidden me in dorms and apartments as I just tried to get through the last semester. I was going home every weekend, and had worked my schedule so I could leave campus at two on Thursday.

The whole fucking reason I was a book narrator was because I could do it from home, I didn't need an employer or a recommendation, or to even talk to anyone from my school to do the job, to get the paycheck.

"Romano!" someone screamed from the end of the row, and a jingle of keys walked down the hall where I couldn't see.

I stood from the bench and walked to the front of the cell. The corrections officer pulled the ring of keys off and unlocked the cell.

"Marcus Romano?"

I nodded.

"Your lawyer is here with your mother."

Shit. *Shit shit shit*. This all over again. So they

could be embarrassed and humiliated. I stepped out into the hallway and he locked the door behind me. He held out the cuff, and I whimpered.

"Can you not put those on me? I puked on shoes from them before."

"Oh, you're the puker. Okay, yeah, fine. They told me you were basically compliant anyway." He motioned me down the cell-line hall and to the door that lead out of the area into the private conference rooms.

My mother was off her feet and pulling me into a huge hug before I was all the way into the room. The correction officer pushed us the rest of the way in and closed the door.

"Marcus—"

"I didn't do shit, Mom," I said.

"I know you didn't," she answered. "I know. This is just college crap all over again." She stepped back and motioned to the two men in the room. "Your boyfriend sent reinforcements."

I laughed. "That's what he said he was going to do."

"Mister Romano, I'm Vincent Bertrand. This is Kyle Tormundsen. Chase—that is, Mister Garcia—has retained us to represent you in this matter."

Shaking the proffered hands, we all sat down around the small table there. Both men were already holding copies of the warrant. I saw a police report on the table, and what looked like a witness statement.

Kyle tossed a look at Vincent. "So, we're going to—"

Holding up my hand, I stopped him. "I have not yet heard the full charges against me from New York and Kings County and by whom. Could we start there?"

"They didn't—" Kyle scribbled something down, and nudged Vincent.

Unfolding the warrant, Vincent sighed and read what was there. "You're being charged with Rape in the First Degree, Criminal Sexual Act in the First Degree, and Predatory Sexual Assault." He pulled out the police report from the pile in front of him. "It says here that Edward George Roberts filed the complaint, on June twenty-fourth, while in care at St. Vincent's hospital. He alleges that you attacked him at the Sonic Boom Studios in—"

My mother held up a hand. "Ed Roberts?"

"That's the name, yes."

My mother stood up and punched the wall. She managed to dent the wallboard, and make both Vincent and Kyle jump. She turned back around and sat. "You need to contact Giles Heurbach, in Boston. He'll have a file you need—all about the last time Ed Roberts pulled this horseshit on my son."

I laid my hand over hers. "Mom."

"I'm not going through this again."

"Neither am I," I said. I turned back to the two lawyers. "My mother will give you the name of the lawyer in Boston, and you can read over the files. Could you please read what he alleges happened?"

"That when you were alone in your studio with him, you raped and beat him."

Mom snorted. "Oh, and beat him now..."

"Mom. Stop. Let me deal with this," I snapped. "He went to the hospital?"

"Two days later. It says here he was ashamed he had been raped by a man." Vincent looked up, and stared at me. "There is a list of his injuries. I have to tell you, Marcus. This is pretty damning stuff."

I folded my hands. "This isn't the first time he's tried this."

"What?" Kyle's head snapped up.

"That's why you need to talk to Mister Heurbach. He handled this last time," I answered. "You'll also need to contact the state police offices, but you'll find there's an order of restraint out, for me against him. The judge granted ten years, and it's only been six."

Vincent leaned forward. "I know Kyle doesn't ask this, but I do. I have one question for you before we move forward another inch. Are you guilty of this in any form."

"No." The answer was simple. "Not even a little." I sighed. "I went to great lengths to avoid him at the studio. Jerry put a rider on the contract that he and I should never be in the building at the same time, and that if we found we were, one of us was to leave immediately. I always did. I was not going to let him get the upper hand."

Vincent was scribbling furiously on his legal pad and Kyle was tapping a finger on this chin. "The reports here are pretty damning, Mister Romano. I have to be honest."

"I expect no less," I answered. "I am innocent."

"I don't think Chase would have asked Vincent if you weren't."

There was a sob next to me, and I looked over to find my mother broken down in tears. "Please, please don't let them put him in jail. This man is a monster and a bully. Marcus hasn't done anything wrong. He never did anything wrong. His only crime is being gay, and that's only in Roberts' eyes."

She grabbed my hand and squeezed.

Kyle cleared his throat, and Vincent spoke up. "Are you saying this is a bullying or hate crime related attack on you? Slander and libel?"

"I don't know what that hospital report says," I answered, "but I personally never laid a finger on him at all."

Tapping the paper, Kyle leaned back. "This is a full evaluation of Ed Roberts, two nights after he claims you raped and beat him. He has physical damage, including a bruised throat."

Mom made a gross sound, but I patted her hand. "You're going to hear worse, Mom. This is Ed."

"So we want to get you out of here. You're not a flight risk, we've convinced the DA of that," Vincent said. "Would you be willing to wear an ankle monitor? I'm not sure we can get the DA to just agree to bail."

"Damfrey knows you're in a bad place to be in gen pop on Riker's," Kyle said. "They do bad things to gay men. Especially one who is on a rape charge."

"If an ankle monitor keeps the cuffs off and keeps me out of a holding cell, yes," I said. "House arrest?"

"No, just an ankle monitor and bail."

Mom leaned forward. "What's bail?"

"Seventy-five thousand," Vincent said. "We might be able to get it reduced if you have a record of showing up for your previous court appearances."

My mother choked and tears rolled down her face. "I don't have that. I don't have it. I have to find a bail bondsman."

The door behind me opened, and we all turned to see Chase walk in, suited and tied and polished. He moved to the corner and looked at the two men. "Repeat the bail amount?"

Vincent sighed. "Seventy-five thousand."

"Check, or do they want a bond?"

I whipped around and stared at him. "Chase!"

He stared me down and repeated the question. "Check, or bond?"

"Bond," Kyle said. "If it was a few thousand less, I'd be okay with a check. But it's a lot of money. Can you get one?"

He pulled out his phone and tapped out a message quickly. "Done. It'll be here in under an hour."

"Good, excellent," Kyle said. "I'm going to go get some of this paperwork going, and request these documents from Massachusetts." Kyle stood and put a hand on my shoulder. "Marcus, my goal is to get this dismissed and expunged. There's no reason for an innocent man to suffer any of this."

"Thank you." My voice was shaking.

He marched out and Vincent let out a breath. We all looked at him, and he blushed bright red. He cleared his throat. "I...uh...I'm not used to working with him. Just against him. But he's the best across the aisle, and I know that you wouldn't ask me for help if you weren't serious, Chase." He closed the folder and shoved it inside his small over the shoulder portfolio. "I have things to do as well. Kyle will be back to get you out of here and Chase will give you my office address so we can get going on this."

Nodding, I stood and shook his hand. "Thank you. Vincent. I know you don't know me from Dick, but I appreciate this."

"Any friend of Chase's is a friend of mine." Politely nodding at my mother, he moved out of the room, and closed the door.

"Chase!" Mom yelled, making us both jump. "A check for bail that big?"

"Yes," he said. "I'm not letting my boyfriend stay in Rikers." He pulled up a chair and sat down. "Can you explain what's going on? Why is someone accusing you of rape?"

I grabbed the copy of the reports that Kyle had left behind, and spun them so Chase could see them. "He's not just accusing me. He's doctoring the evidence. I'm hoping that once these cops look at this, the whole case falls apart."

✩

CHASE

THE PICTURES on the table were no fucking joke. They were of a man who was beaten badly, and...well.

Clearly had been penetrated.

Dawn stood. "I'll let him tell you the story, I can't hear it again. I'm going to get some fresh air."

Marcus nodded and waited until the officer outside let her out.

As soon as the door closed, I grabbed Marcus and pulled him to me for a hug. "Damn it," I hissed. "I am so sorry my brother did this. He's been ejected from the house. Mom won't let him back." I leaned back and looked him up and down. "Are you all right?"

He ran a hand down his face, then shook his head. "No. I don't think I am. Chase, I can't afford two lawyers, and I don't have the money to pay you back for this bail. I just don't. I appreciate what you're doing—"

Pulling him to me again, I slanted my mouth over his and kissed him hard. "Did you mean it?"

He went red from his toes to the top of his hair, then ducked his head. I grabbed his chin and lifted him to look at me. "Did you?"

Marcus' eyes welled with tears. "I...yeah. Yes. I did. I do. I'd been kind of thinking about it a bit, but after it slipped out, I really felt it." He leaned forward and whispered against my lips, "I love you, Chase."

I kissed him back, softly, slowly, sweetly. "I love you, Marcus. Please, tell me what happened here so we can get you out and get home and celebrate that."

"You may not want to after you hear this."

I put my hand on his cheek. "Did you hurt someone? Did you kill someone? Did you rape or abuse anyone?"

"God no!"

"Then, nothing is going to change my mind. Tell me. And I'll tell you why I can afford Kyle Tormundsen."

His eyebrow rose. "Bribery, sir?"

"Damn skippy, and I'm tossing in some sex for the hell of it."

Turning solemn, almost sullen, Marcus sat back in his chair and folded his arms. "So...I got accepted to Boston Conservatory for a whole host of things. I got in on visual arts, vocal arts, and classical guitar."

"You play—"

"Nothing and I'll explain why in a minute." He took a deep breath. "I started dating Ed Roberts in my junior year. He was not an ideal boyfriend, and I should have realized what was up ages before the incidents. But I wanted the support of a *boyfriend* and he was there. Too there, if you know what I mean. Pushing me to go out with him, always at my rehearsals and recitals. I thought it would be fine once I got used to him. And you, of all people, know that *getting used to* someone is a bad sign. I wasn't that smart.

"We started dating in October, and by February we were always together. He moved me into his apartment and started isolating me. I was smart enough to see that coming, though, and about four weeks after I moved in, I moved back out, telling him I just wasn't ready.

"April was already heavy rehearsal season for the upper classmen, and I pushed through, relieved to go home for the summer.

"When I got back the next year, my senior year, people who had been kind of friendly were giving me looks that would take a SCUD missile down midflight. Some of the people I had called almost friends were avoiding me. Some of the friends Ed and I shared were now fully and only his. And of course, I had no idea what was going on."

Marcus shook his head and I could see he was having trouble talking. I scooted my chair closer and took his hand in both of mine. I wasn't going to push him for the story, but he started up again in a moment.

"During the course of the summer, he'd started a rumor I had been abusing him. That he had kicked me out of the apartment after I'd wormed my way in. And about mid-October, I'd had enough and I wanted it over with. I asked him nicely to meet me in the library and we could talk this out and be done.

"I was arrested a week later. Suspicion of rape. Ed had filed the report on me saying I had raped him in the library. The spot he said I did it was one of the few not covered by a camera.

"My parents had to drain their savings to get me out of it. The lawyers, the bail, the civil suit. God, they had to bond their house to get me out. Roberts' family was wealthy and had the ear of a lot of the Boston elite. I was so close to screwed.

"Someone, somewhere decided to set the Roberts family to rights, though, and we pulled the best judge we could hope for. Judge Helen Allen. She heard the evidence, she heard how my story never changed. She listened when I told my side of the story. She directed that courtroom like one of the conductors at the school. And the jury came back with a not guilty. She ordered the ten year restraining order, and I was released. All bail monies released, and bond paid. Lawyer paid. It was over."

Marcus stopped again, and I pulled one of the bottles of water over to us, cracking the top open for him. He took a hard pulled on it, and I could tell he wished it was whiskey or maybe even the sterno.

"It wasn't over, was it?" I asked quietly.

"Not by a fucking long shot."

I waited, and after another drink of water, Marcus went on.

"I lost all but a few of my friends. My roommate beat the shit out of me on the first day back to classes. I never knew he had a brown belt in Okinawan karate. I did after that night. I had to go to the ER, which was fun. *My twink roommate decided that I was a rapist and laid into me, a massive linebacker.* Size does not trump skill. Ever.

"I started couch surfing among the few friends I still had. They were happy to pass me along between them, and I only went back to my very expensive dorm room when I knew my roommate was out. I made sure I orchestrated the last semester so I would only be on campus three nights, and home the rest of the time. Four and a half hours back and forth every weekend.

"Even some of the teachers had turned on me, and I could barely pass their classes, tests, and recital panels. But. My guitar teacher never did. He arranged for an audition for a small but well-paying classical group, and I went in December.

"Ed and his groupies met me outside the audition after I had given a flawless performance. Best of my life. I had nailed it, perfect. Every note, every beat.

"After his cronies smashed my guitar, they held me against the wall. Ed grabbed a brick and smashed my left hand. The one that sat on the fingerboard, that made the chords and notes. He kept smashing it. Six times. Four with the flat of it and two with the edge."

Marcus held up his left hand. "Looks good, doesn't it?" He put it on the table in front of him. "I spent the rest of December and all of January in the hospital. I had an external fixator, like I was fucking Doctor Strange. The bones healed. There are small pins in some of them. I spent two years relearning how to use my fingers. And for the most part they work. But they were never strong enough, nimble enough again, to play the guitar."

He lifted his ring finger above the others. For the first time, I saw the tiny round scar there. "Fixator scar. I was able to minimize all of them with wound care." He curved them and the held them there. Not fifteen seconds later, they started trembling. "That's it. That's all I have. That's all the strength I have. I can type, because the keys are so light now. But the guitar?" He let out a breath.

"I spent my last semester of college learning all the sound tech shit I could cram in my brain, and made sure that my voice lessons were on track and on campus during the middle of the day."

"Did you ever find out why he did all this?"

Marcus nodded, slowly, sadly. "He was jealous. He'd heard me play, and he knew that he didn't have the talent I had. He didn't have a chance at being a professional beyond some cheap jazz clubs. In all the months we were together, I had *no idea* he played. I never saw him practice, not once. I thought he was there for sound production alone. He didn't practice, as it turned out. He had a natural talent, but he never did anything with it.

"I'd been playing since I was seven. Guitar was my backup for my vocal career. I was good. Fucking good. Then it was gone.

"I can't even enjoy messing around with the fucking thing because I can't use my fucking hands that way anymore. He took that from me, and now he's back. He's going to take more away from me. My job, my ability to live my life.

"Everything is going backward, Chase. I worked so hard to get where I am. I deserved that award last year. Now it's all in retrograde. My whole life is spinning backward."

I wrapped my hands around the nape of his neck

and pulled him close, leaning his forehead on mine. "You know what's good about retrograde? It only appears to be spinning backward. Eventually, the illusion stops and everything starts moving in the right orbit again. I want to be that orbit, Marcus. And I want you to be mine."

He burst into wracking sobs, and I just held him.

CHAPTER TWENTY-TWO

MARCUS

I DRAGGED MY ASS TO THE DOOR of my apartment and let out a sigh. "I'll see you in the—"

Chase spun me around and kissed me hard. "No. You're coming in here with me and I'm going to fuck you senseless and you're going to realize that you're not doing this alone."

"I have my parents—"

"Who can't stay down here because they have a life upstate," he said, taking my elbow and pulling me toward his apartment. "They love you, Marcus, and they will stand behind you. But I love you too, and I want to help you."

"You have already," he said.

He pulled me in close so his next words ghosted over his lips. "Not the way I wanted to, I can't do that in public."

The door opened and MC was there nuzzling the wall next to us as we walked in. My mother popped out of the kitchen, holding a chicken pot pie. The place was clean and organized and smelled like...

Home. It smelled like a place I wanted to spend the rest of my life.

God, I was *not* going to fucking cry again.

I took a minute for myself, and ducked into the bathroom, just to wash my face and compose myself. It felt natural to be in Chase's space, and I liked that. It felt as natural as being in the old house in Troy.

"Marcus Chastain, come eat and be social."

I laughed. Mom was a balm for my tired soul. How at twenty-eight was I this exhausted?

She'd left as soon as Vin and Kyle had confirmed the bond was set and the corrections department was on their way to buckle the damn ankle monitor on. They programmed it so I could walk the dog, go to the vet, the grocery store, and work. Anything outside those parameters was grounds for being hauled back in unless I could prove that it was an emergency.

Dawn Romano thought that food solved all problems. While it didn't, not really, I was not one to turn down the pure country gourmet of her chicken pot pie.

Pure country gourmet meaning about four thousand calories a bite. It had been my go-to in high school for bulking up. I didn't need that anymore, but there was more to it than calories. There was love, and caring, and mouthfuls of pure deliciousness.

We sat around the table, scooping out the deliciousness on to our plates, and my mother pulled out three beers and put them in front of each plate. "We all need those," she said, sitting down.

"We sure do," I said, swiping it and taking a hardy gulp.

She pushed her chicken, carrots, and crust around the plate. "Chase, I spoke to my husband when I got back here earlier and we'd like to work out a repayment schedule with you for the lawyers."

"Nope," he said, simply.

"Chase, this is a lot of money. We had to bond our house last time. I know what—"

"No. No repayment. This is me taking care of my boyfriend," he said, and put the fork down. "It's not going to dent the bank account. At all. Let me pay for it."

"Chase," I said, "I appreciate that, but I agree with my mother. We need to work out a repayment schedule."

Casually chewing his dinner, he pulled out his phone and flipped to some app deep in the folders and collections on the screen. He popped it open, and tapped in a few numbers, navigating through the information. Finally, he settled on something and dropped the phone face up between me and my mother.

I looked at the screen, and then up at Chase, to my mother, and back to the screen.

"That's a fucking load of numbers, Chase..." I whispered.

"A load of them," my mother echoed. "All in front of a decimal."

He pulled it back. "That's just my money market. Would you like to see the checking? The savings? The stocks?" Fingers flew over the front closing things and opening others.

I slipped my hand over the screen. "Stop, Chase."

"I don't need the money back," he said. "I don't even need to work. But what the hell am I going to do with my free time? Coke and whores?"

Choking on the carrot I was trying to chew, I stared at him wide eyed. My mother started laughing.

"Was that actually an option?"

"No, not really. I was too busy trying to figure what the hell to do with all the money," Chase said.

"Where did it come from?" I asked. "I mean, your parents' farm is fantastic, and does well, but it's not a money maker. Not like that."

Chase put his fork down and flipped through his phone again. "When I first got here to the city I had no money, no friends, and a scholarship to Cooper Union. That was it. So I took a job as a home health aide. I did the evening shift, and I was assigned to a man named Martin Marsden. He was an older man, with advanced ALS and a serious bug up his ass. But I stuck it out. I needed the money and he would always need an aide."

He put the phone down and turned it so we could look at it. It was an old picture of an older man with a ton of white hair and a laugh on his face, sitting in a very advanced looking wheelchair.

"I eventually broke through his shit attitude and started to get to the real Martin. He was a nice guy, dealt a shit hand in life. Only child of only children, he'd lost his wife young. There were no children. He'd had a lot of friends over the years, but he was it now. Once the ALS had started to steal his life, he got pissed and curled in on himself.

"He hired me on full time, and contracted with a day nurse to help me while I was in school. But I moved in with him and we basically became each other's family. He was a good guy and once we started to get to know each other I dragged him to Central Park and a few museums and I made sure that we ate out once in a while. About once a week.

"But finally, toward the end of my junior year, it was clear that the ALS was getting the better of him. We had to move him out of his apartment into a nursing home. I was still there, every day, checking on him, talking with him.

"Before he went in, he created a living will, stating that when he was no longer able to breathe on his own, he didn't want to be dependent on the vent. He agreed to go on it, but when it was clear that it was only the vent keeping him alive, he wanted to be taken off.

"And within a few months of moving into the place, he was moved to the vent full time, and he made me remind them of his will. He wanted it carried out. He was only on the vent for two weeks when the judge agreed that the will stood."

I saw Chase let out a breath. He'd really been this guy's family when he needed it. And Martin had been there for him when he had nothing.

"It was me, two nurses, and one of his very old coworkers at his funeral. That was it. He really had no one. I made sure he was buried with his wife, and went back to the apartment we'd shared to button it up and move out. I'd already found this place—" he waved his hand around "—at a decent price. I'd planned to have a roommate.

"The lawyer called me the next week, to come to his office. I had no idea. I thought maybe I had screwed up somehow or I had to be out of the apartment before my new place was ready."

I scooped up a bit of the chicken pie. "That wasn't it at all, was it?" I shoved the spoon in my mouth.

"Not even close," he said. "Martin Masden had been a high-powered Wall Street broker in the mid-80s, through the death of his wife in 1995. He made a metric shit ton of money. He invested wisely, conservatively, and broadly. And by the time he died, he had nearly fifty million dollars to his name.

"And he left it all to me."

"Shit," Mom said.

"Yeah." Chase nodded. "I've left it basically untouched. I use some of it to pay for this place, because let's face it, graphic designers at my level aren't rolling in cash but I adore what I do. Otherwise...it just sits there."

My mother whacked my arm. "You put 1500 miles on my car when you could have rented a Lear jet to Illinois."

"How the hell was I supposed to know the guy was a millionaire?"

Chase laughed. "I'll buy you a new car."

Mom turned and pointed at him. "Don't you dare. You take care of my son. If you're willing to spend that money on him, then you do that, keep him out of jail and safe, and pay for my oil change."

I STARED down at the ankle monitor and its once-a-minute blinking green light. I hated it, but at the same time, it was my stay out of jail for now card.

Chase climbed into the bed and snuggled against me.

"Stop staring at it. We'll have it off soon. Roberts is a piece of shit, and we'll be able to prove that he was lying."

"Those pictures are pretty convincing," I mumbled.

"Plain old rough sex could do that," he said. "You can trust me on that."

"Mm. Yeah, I know."

He snorted. "Yeah. There's always that one."

"Jeeze, yes. The experimenter," I answered. "Balls deep no lube. I was ready to buy a hemorrhoid donut the next day."

Chuckling, his fingers circled on my skin, dipping below the waist of my boxers. "You're lucky. I know what I'm doing."

"Oh, do you?"

"I do," he whispered. "Would you like a demonstration?"

"Perhaps I do," I answered.

He leaned up and kissed the side of my mouth with clear intent. "Your ass is mine, Marc. Tonight, it's my turn, and you need someone to take care of you."

"I—"

He put a finger over my lips. "I told you I switch, and I want to make you feel good." Moving his finger, he leaned down and kissed me—languid and without demand. It was so careful and so full of love, it almost scared me.

Because every drop of love he gave to me, I gave back. This man had my heart.

He leaned to the nightstand and grabbed the condom and lube and dropped them on the blanket next to us.

"Let me play?" he asked quietly.

"Of course," I answered. I regretted the allowance almost immediately because in seconds I thought the man was going to kill me as he sucked one of my nipples into his mouth and rolled the other in his fingers.

And then I nearly died when I felt his finger graze over my hole. He stroked carefully, softly, a feathery touch that had me squirming and gasping and grabbing his hair.

He nibbled and licked his way down my body, twirling his tongue around my cock, licking his way up, and over and down, all while that finger teased me.

The man had me shaking and sweating.

He swallowed me whole and hummed while I was deep in his throat, forcing a stuttering gasp out of me that I had never heard before.

But instead of continuing there, he let me pop out of his mouth with a dirty sound, and went back to his journey down my body. His fist wrapped around my erection instead of playing at my nipples, but it wasn't a hard grip, and not very serious.

Because in the next moment, his tongue circled around my balls and pulled one delicate orb into his mouth. He hummed again and it became very clear to me why all this was called a hummer.

Hot summer lightning raced up my spine and spiked in my brain. The climax was growing—and he had me leaping ahead when he switched to the other side of my sac.

"Shit," I managed to hiss.

He pulled away and I wanted to beg him to come back and finish me. My dick was aching it was so hard, and I needed the relief.

And then he made me slap my hands over my mouth to keep the scream from echoing in the building—his tongue found the sensitive skin of my hole and danced over it. I could feel his smile on my skin, his lazy hand on my erection.

Chase feasted on me. I wanted more. I wrapped my hands around the back of my knees and pulled myself up and open for him.

"Greedy," he whispered, the sensation of his hot breath making me gasp again.

"Fuck yes I am," I answered, but I wasn't sure that's what came out of my mouth. I was pretty sure it was a line of incomprehensible gobbledygook.

He teased me, tracing over me time and again and then dipped inside me. I had to let go of one of my legs and cover my mouth again. This man was determined to make me scream and wake the building.

The cap on the lube snapped open and I was ready to tell him to call 911, because I was having the best death ever.

His tongue moved out of the way of his finger as he slipped it inside. There was a little burn, but he managed to find my prostate right away. I was near tears from the pleasure.

"No—Jesus, Joseph and Jehoshaphat, get your dick in me, Chase!" I cried.

His hand was gone from my cock and I heard the foil rip as he looked up at me. "You sure?"

"Oh, shit in Shinola, if you don't get in me, I'm going to blow without you."

"I should take more time..."

"No, Chase, no, fuck me already!"

He smirked as he rolled the condom on, spreading some more lube on himself and drizzling a few cold drops on my hole. Before I could yell at him again, he pressed himself against me and pushed lightly.

I should have let him stretch me more, but I just needed to feel him inside. The burn was uncomfortable, but he was slow, steady, and careful as he pushed in. He stopped when I grimaced, without me saying a thing, and finally, I felt his plump balls pressed against the flesh of my ass. He felt so fucking good, and I felt so fucking full of Chase.

Leaning forward, he pressed his lips to mine, and I could taste the faint dusky remains of me on his lips. I had never really liked that before, but this time...it was Chase, and I liked the way I tasted on his mouth.

"Good?" he asked.

"Move, please."

He did. I bit the side of my hand.

Chase laughed and leaned to my ear. "You need a gag."

"Oh...*fuck*." The very idea of this man tying me up

made my dick jump between us.

At first he was slow, letting me stretch around him. But, it didn't take long for me to get there, and we could both feel the moment my body agreed to this, agreed to let him shuttle his dick in and out of me.

So he did. Hard and fast, glancing off that spot inside that made me see stars every time.

I was going to pass out. I could see the flashes of light in my head, warning lights, that I was going to crash and pass out.

Wrapping his hand around me, wet with a little lube, he stroked me at the same pace his stroked in and out of my ass. His fist was tight, then loose, then tight—

"I'm coming," I gasped as he tightened once more.

"Let me see it, baby," he growled. "Let me see you come on your chest. Show me."

The orgasm exploded from the tip of my cock, the tacky cum flying up onto my stomach, my chest, even my neck. The lights behind my eyes were like strobes, and my ears were ringing.

My hole clenched hard on Chase, and just as I looked up at him, he came. It was a glorious sight to see that pleasure rippling through him as he spilled his own seed in the condom. "*Marcus!*"

His forehead touched mine and we were panting in time with each other, letting the climax roll through me. It took a while before he opened his eyes and grinned at me.

"Holy hell," he breathed.

"You ain't kidding," I answered, pulling him down onto me, ignoring the sticky mess between us.

"I like switching with you," he murmured, licking a little of the cum from my neck.

"I could tell."

Chuckling, he pulled himself up and slipped himself free of my body. Condom gone, lube back in the drawer, and both of us wiped clean from the climax, he crawled up next to me on the bed, and snuggled into my arms.

"Marcus?"

"Yeah, babe?"

"Can we just get tested and ditch the condoms?"

"Shit yes," I answered.

"Good," he mumbled, drifting off. "Love you."

"Love you right back."

☆

I REACHED down and scratched the ankle monitor. I had to remember to use an alcohol wipe under it later. I could shower with it, but it was fastened tight.

Sorcha gave me a side long glance and sighed.

"You okay?"

"Fuck no." The words were out before I could stop them. Letting out a blast of frustrated breath, I sank a bit in the chair. "No. I'm not okay. Please, for the love of all that's holy and unholy in the afterlife, tell me you believe me."

"Believe you?"

"That I didn't rape him."

"Oh, yeah. Of course, I believe you. You didn't even have to ask. That guy has given me the hee-bee gee-bees since he walked into the conference room.

The fact that he was always trying to get you alone was another one. Oh, also a big clue? Restraining order written into the rider on the contract."

She slid a few of the controls around. "He's a bully, isn't he?"

"Bully would be kind," I said. "He's one of the most awful people you ever wanted to meet. He's a good sound producer, but not great and if it wasn't for his family, he would have been working backstage at some rinky dink community theater in Omaha."

"And away from you and your magnificent vocals."

I turned my head slowly and looked at her. "What?"

She glanced up at the ceiling. "What did he call it? Oh, yeah, your *fuck me* bedroom voice."

My jaw dropped open. "You...talked to Chase."

"He was here this morning to talk to all of us with those two delicious and very gay lawyers he hired for you." She pressed a few buttons and hit a key on the computer. "They're hot for each other."

"Uh, Kyle and Vincent?" I asked. "No, not really. Kyle just railroads over Vin and they end up arguing. A lot. Like more than normal and—wait." I considered what I had just said, and shook my head, then smirked. "You're right. They are hot for each other."

Sorcha laughed. "I like them though. They're good lawyers. And I suspect..." Her eyes darted to me and back. "I suspect they work like their own detective team and the two of them are going to make sure you're not just freed, but completely cleared, and possibly turning this back on What's His Face."

"What's His Face that destroyed my life."

Sorcha put a hand on my arm. "He didn't. You know he didn't. He changed it. Not destroyed it. Don't give him the mental space, that power over you. You have Chase in your life now, and all those wacky nuts he calls friends. You have a dog that loves you, and you saved kittens from a wall. I promise, you are not destroyed."

I stared at the knobs on the board, and nodded. "I'm not destroyed. I am rebuilt. I'm reinforced."

"Also, there are enough holes in Roberts' story to drive an earthmover through. The ones they use in mining? With the massive wheels and you have to climb a ladder to get into? Yeah. Those."

I cracked up laughing. "I just hope everyone can see that."

"They will."

The phone on the table next to her rang and she hit the speaker. "Sorcha."

"Hey, it's Jerry. Come up to the conference room. They want to talk about the tracks on the show."

She shot a look at me. "Is he going to be there?"

"No," Jerry said.

"We'll be up in a minute," I answered.

Sorcha disconnected and saved the work on the clip. We headed up to the conference room, where Jerry was sitting with Raph.

"Good. I have no idea why they pulled this impromptu meeting, but I'm not happy," Jerry said. "We have a lot of work we need to get done, and this is a waste of time."

"Totally agreed," Sorcha said, taking the seat next

to Raph.

I walked around and stood on Jerry's other side. "Hate me?"

"Fuck you, Romano. Sit your ass down. I do not hate you. No one does. I know you rescue kittens from walls."

"I do," I said with a sigh, sinking into the chair. I scratched at the monitor again. "Never thought I'd have to wear one of these things."

Jerry shrugged. "Make sure you not only wipe under it, but get some moisturizer in the skin. It'll chafe otherwise."

Me, Raph, and Sorcha were all staring at him. He darted his eyes to each of us. "What? Those stupid things chafe."

"You?"

"Of course," he said. "I did eight months on one of those for some car theft. Years ago. Third strike shit. Never steal wheels from cars that are parked in your neighbor's yard."

"Wow, the truth comes out." Sorcha laughed. "Jerry is our resident thief."

"Jerry is your resident former thief who basically got schooled that a life of crime is not for him," he said, raising an eyebrow. "But I was guilty, and our boy here is not."

I thumped him on the back. "Thanks, man."

The door opened and the producers of the show walked in, chatting among themselves.

In the middle was Ed Roberts.

Jerry toss his chair back as he stood and pointed at him. "*I told you not to bring him in here!*" His voice roared through the conference room and halted everyone in their place. "Get out. Get out of here!"

Raph had the phone off the hook and I could see the question in his eyes. *Security or police?* I glanced at him and hopefully he got my message. *Security.*

Sorcha was around the chairs and had pressed herself up against my shoulder where I sat. I could see the fury in her eyes as well. "Get out of here."

"He's the sound producer—" one of the other jerks said.

"There is a restraining order on him for not less than one hundred yards!" Jerry snapped. "He has moved into the space and we could have him arrested. Get him out of here."

A cruel look spread across Ed's face and every ounce of hatred I'd ever had for him boiled up. I was shaking with rage. He'd done this on purpose. He wanted me rattled, he wanted me to make a stupid move. I calmly stood from the chair and looked at Jerry.

He nodded. Sorcha nodded. Even Raph nodded.

Sorcha wrapped her arms around my shoulders and guided me around the table toward the door. The security guards scooted up the hall and stopped just behind the group. They bodily shoved everyone in the door out of the way and held them back while Sorcha guided me through the door.

Ed actually had the balls to reach for me.

Sorcha grabbed his hand and twisted, pinching the bundle of nerves between his thumb and index finger bringing him to his knees with a screech.

"You were told not to come in, you were told to

leave twice. You *violated* the rider on the contract that your company signed." She spit the words at him. "You deserve so much worse than a pinch and kneel."

Releasing him, she joined me with the one guard and we scrambled out of there, up the stairs into Jerry's office and Violet nodded at us. "Good choice. The cops are on their way."

"Who called—"

"I did," she said. "I'm not stupid. The security guys are good, but we can get this on record, terminate the contract and not lose a penny."

Sorcha and I stared at her, and her eyebrow lifted a moment later. "What? You think Jerry keeps me around for my effervescent personality? Hell no. I'm a hound at contract law, too."

She pulled the door closed and smiled.

"I cannot believe he tried to grab you!"

"I can," I said. I leaned against the door in the back and sighed. "He's trying to get me to fuck up. And someone on his team is on his side. We have to find out who it was that Jerry talked to."

"*I told you, Menendez! I didn't want him in here.*"

Sorcha lifted her brow and stared at me "You heard that, right?"

"Yeah... What the hell?"

"*You can't tell me who on my team can come and go here. This contract is millions, Liggit. Millions. We own your ass.*"

"*No one owns my ass, Menendez!*"

"Where is that coming from?" I hissed. "Why can we hear something going on two floors down?"

Sorcha was staring at me. Or I thought she was,

but a second later realized she was staring at the door. I gasped and turned around, staring at it. I turned the knob and the door opened.

We stepped inside to find a bank of computers and displays.

They were full of all the goings on in the studios.

Sorcha shared my look, and her jaw unhinged. Lunging for the keyboard, she quickly studied the monitors and found the one with the conference room on it. She brought up a menu, and had that feed show up on the big screen.

"Oh...my God. How did we not realize this was here?" My voice was hoarse.

Sorcha stared at the equipment. "I thought this was a closet!"

"You brought in Roberts after I had it in the rider that you couldn't without twenty-four hours notice!" Jerry was turning red with anger. *"He just tried to grab my employee!"*

"Your rider is ridiculous—"

"Menendez, shut up."

I gasped at who had spoken. "Was he in there when we were?"

"No! He came in after. Holy shit," Sorcha gasped. "Nelson *fucking* Powers."

"Sir, this is—"

"I said, shut up, Menendez. I'm talking to Mister Liggit now. The rider on the contract was for...?"

"Mister Romano has a restraining order on Mister Roberts, and the rider was designed to keep both of them safe, by providing a time frame for us to make alternate arrangements for our employee.

That was violated today."

"Get Roberts out of here."

"Sir—"

Powers started swearing... I didn't even know what language that was at first, but eventually I realized it was freakin' Icelandic. Quickly, he realized what he was doing and switched back to English. *"Get. Him. Out."*

Menendez turned to Roberts and nodded. With an audible sniff, he turned and walked out of the room.

The wrong direction.

"Follow him..." I whispered.

Sorcha and I turned back to the massive bank of monitors and watched him walked through the halls, down the stairs, and through the studio level below the conference room. He peered into other studios, opened doors, and finally found my studio.

Roberts jimmied it open, and grinned.

"Shit, we need better security," Sorcha whispered.

"What the hell is he doing? What is he doing in my office. Are there anymore cameras?"

Sorcha started typing like mad, and sorting through the screens she was on. She read menus as fast as she could, and yelped in triumph a moment later.

There on the big screen in front of her, appeared the inside of my studio in a fish-eye lens.

She gasped, "It's already recording."

"Oh, my God..." I breathed. Could they actually have the recordings of all of our interactions?

"What is he doing?" Sorcha moved closer to the

screen.

I watched the scene in front of me, and saw what she was talking about. He was wiping a finger down his cheek, then pressing it to various surfaces. After about two minutes of that, he pulled something out of his pocket, and crawled under the soundboard, all the way underneath. He disappeared for about ten seconds then crawled back out. Pressing a few more oily fingers around the room, including grabbing the chair with both hands, he seemed satisfied with whatever the hell he was doing and walked back out into the corridor.

"Holy shit," she breathed. "I'll bet a dollar he just planted evidence."

"Didn't they already search my studio?"

"I don't know..." She stared at the screen, and a second later, a grin spread across her face. "But we can find out, can't we." Picking up the phone, she quickly dialed a number, watching me as someone picked up on the other end. "Hey, Raph. Yeah, can you come up to Jerry's office? We have something we need your help with..."

CHAPTER

TWENTY-THREE

CHASE

KYLE AND VINCENT STOOD WITH MARCUS in the front of the courtroom, heads together chatting with each other. They were *not* comfortable with each other at that moment, and I wanted to laugh at Vincent.

We were here for the preliminary hearing, to see if Ed's accusations were going forward to court. I didn't see how they could, but discovery had brought up all the lurid details of what had happened in Boston to my boyfriend, and that looked bad.

There was new evidence, too, that the prosecutor had shared late. I'd heard Vincent curse the man out just a few minutes before and it had taken all Kyle had to pull the man off the other lawyer.

But now we were settled and waiting for the judge to get back from lunch.

I wanted this shit over with. I knew he wasn't

guilty, and they should just trust me. I sat back and harrumphed like a child, even folding my arms.

Raphael ran in just as the bailiff appeared in the door.

"Got it," he panted and shoved two CDs at them.

"All of it? Like we asked," Vincent said.

Raph nodded. "Just like you asked."

"Good man, take a seat."

"All rise for the Honorable Judge Michael Demico." The bailiff stood at attention while the judge walked in and sat down.

"Be seated," he called.

There was a flurry of shit I didn't understand going on after that. Court documents, timing, reporters, transcriptions, and just all kind of things that didn't make sense to my untrained ears.

What I did see was Marcus sitting quietly with his hands folded. For the first time since I met him, I couldn't read him. I couldn't tell if he was happy, sad, scared...

There was a yelp from the prosecutors table. We all turned to look and found the woman absolutely red-faced and shaking with rage as she stared at something Kyle had handed her just a few minutes before. Her manicured nails cut through the paper and she looked ready to scream.

"Your honor, may I have a ten minute recess." She held up the paper and a CD.

"Objections?" the judge asked.

"No your honor."

"Good." He banged his gavel. "Pee break." He

stood, we stood, he trotted out, and the prosecutor hauled out through the back doors.

Dawn laughed lightly next to me. "I've never heard a judge so informal."

"Old man bladder." Kyle snickered. "He's an amazing judge, but he has no duration."

"Man needs saw palmetto," Vincent mumbled. Kyle laughed, then caught himself and stopped it.

Oh, yeah. They had it bad.

"What did you hand the prosecutor?" Dawn asked.

"Magic," Kyle answered, "in the form of a transcript and a CD."

"Well, I saw that," I said.

"It's our ace in the hole," Vincent said. "What we hope is going to get this whole thing dismissed right here, right now, and that stupid ankle monitor taken off."

"It chafes," Marcus said. "Figuratively and literally."

"I gave you moisturizer," Dawn said.

"Mom? It's an ankle monitor for a criminal. It doesn't matter how much moisturizer I put on. It's always going to chafe. That's kind of the point."

"That's kind of cruel," Dawn said.

"They kind of don't care," Vincent said. "Innocent until proven guilty means nothing to some people." He tossed a meaningful look at Kyle.

Kyle didn't flinch, but his eyes looked hurt.

"We're just going to sit here and wait?" Dawn asked.

"We are," Marcus said. "The information we gave her, and is currently available for the judge to review, should be the end of it."

I pulled out my cell phone and messed around with it, even though it earned me some dirty looks from the officers around. Tough shit—I needed to check the status of work with some of the people on my team, to make sure I didn't have to go into work tonight.

At the nine minute mark, the prosecutor walked back in, her heels making a threatening clack on the floor with each angry step. She didn't head to her own table on the right. Instead, she headed straight for Marcus, Vincent, and Kyle.

"Counselors. A moment?"

The three of them walked off to talk quietly in the corner, and I could see her face go from angry to resigned, and then to her professional neutral and nod once.

The door to the judge's chambers open and the bailiff had to scramble. "All rise!"

We shuffled to our feet, and watched him sit. We sat.

"Your honor," Vincent started. "We have some new evidence we want to present to the court. We want to put this on record."

He nodded.

Kyle walked to the media center the courtroom had and slipped the CD in the player. The bailiff turned down the lights and the CD started playing. The logo of Kyle's firm came up, and out of the corner of my eye, I saw Vincent grouse. After that, you could have put the seal of the office of the president and I wouldn't have cared.

Because the screen was filled with Ed Roberts.

The first clips were of all the times he tried to get Marcus alone. Next were the times he'd managed to do it, and Marcus walked right the hell out of the room. There was one time where he'd stood in front of the door so Marcus couldn't leave. There was the antagonizing catcalls down the hall. The intentional shoves. The pushes. The 'whoops why are you here?' encounters.

And through all of them, Marcus was never in his space for longer than it took to get away.

The piece de resistance, though, was composed of two clips.

In the first, it was just Marcus in his studio. Sitting, working, playing with the soundboard, mixing for the images on the screen in front of us. It sped up, showing hours of work, right through 9:03 p.m. on the night of the attack. The report said he was attacked between eight and nine at night.

The other one was just as damning. Roberts, sneaking into Marcus's studio, planting prints and evidence.

The prints and evidence that were sitting on the table in front of the judge.

The player shut off and the room was quiet for a long moment.

"What is that bullshit!?" Roberts finally roared. "Are you presenting deepfakes as evidence?"

"I have a signed affidavit that these are not deepfakes at all," Vincent said. "They are genuine copies from the hard drive of the security system at Sonic Boom Studios. A system which had not previously been known to us."

"Oh, isn't that convenient!"

"Mrs. Bondano?" the judge said.

"The state withdraws all charges against Mister Marcus Romano, and release all bail holdings. No further actions will be taken against him in this matter."

Dawn slumped against me, and I clutched my hand over my heart. I heard a little cheer go up from the back of the room, and turning to look, found *all* of my friends there. The judge stared at them until they shut up.

"Your honor, you can't do this!" Roberts said. "He violated me!"

Bondano pulled him close and whispered in his ear. Roberts went white. Sheer, terrified white. She motioned to the officers at the back of the room and they marched forward, pulling out their own set of cuffs.

"Mister Roberts, you are hereby placed under arrest for planting evidence, making a false police report and misdemeanor falsification of hospital records," the one said. "I'm sure that Mrs. Bondano has more for you, too."

He turned and narrowed his eyes at Marcus. "You lousy asshole! Why didn't you just die? Why couldn't you just fucking go away forever! You're not worth shit to anyone! You always had to be better than me! Even after I smashed your fucking hand, you had to outdo me!"

Marcus turned and stared at Roberts. "I didn't know you from a hole in the wall, Ed. And I would have happily let you live in obscurity. You're nothing to me, you were nothing to me, and now...you can go be someone's bitch on Rikers and die in obscurity."

"I'll fucking kill you!"

"Add that to your list?" Marcus looked at Bondano, who had to school her laugh, and managed a nod.

"Mister Romano, if you'll see the officers in the room across the hall, we'll get that ankle monitor off you and you can signed the paperwork for the release of bail, and to clear your records. I hope you continue on the path of a law abiding citizen and won't be swayed by this misdirection of justice."

"No, your honor, I'm not swayed," Marcus said. "Thank you, sir."

He picked up the gavel and smacked it once. "Case dismissed. Ten minute recess for the next case."

Marcus walked around the railing, grabbed me from where I had stood after the judge walked out, and kissed me stupid. "Thank you."

"For what?"

"For believing me," he said.

I put my hand on his cheek. "I love you, dumb ass. Of course I believe you."

Dawn suddenly had both arms around us and squeezed us tight. "My boys will be home without the man watching them tonight! We need to go out to eat somewhere fancy!"

"Can we do delicious instead?" I asked. "Because I'm thinking Eataly."

She grabbed me away from Marcus and planted a kiss on each cheek. "You are a marvel. Yes! Italian!"

The group of us headed to the back of the room where my—*our* friends were waiting. Before we could get there though, something tall and dark and forbiddenly sexy stepped into our path.

Marcus and I looked up.

Nelson Powers.

"Nelson Powers..." he breathed.

"Mister Romano, I would like to apologize on behalf of my production company," he said.

I was only able to half hear his words because *Nelson Fucking Powers in gray pinstripes talking to me. To* my boyfriend. Technicality.

"Mister Powers, it was nothing to do with you."

"No, I've fired the sound producers," he said, slicing into Marcus' words. "I've already spoke to Jerry Liggit, but I wanted to tell you as well. They're fired. I'd like to bring on Sonic Boom as our main sound production for this show."

"Sir?"

"It's Nelson." He smirked. "But yes. I'll expect you in the meeting next week to get the contracts up. I do apologize for this. Ed Roberts had been coasting on his family name. And I don't abide people who do that. You can have a famous name, but don't coast on it. Work for it." He patted Marcus on the shoulder.

"Also, I adored your reading of *Too Far the Near Shore.*" He leaned in. "And that lovely shorter work, *The Man for Me.*"

Nelson *fucking* Powers shook my hand, turned to our group of friends, tossed them a wink and was out the door.

"Nelson Powers touched my son..." Dawn whispered.

I grabbed his hand, the one that Nelson's hand shook. "Oh, no you don't. This hand is mine. I have plans."

MARCUS SCRATCHED the spot where the monitor had just been removed. We were signing a ton of papers so he could be free and clear and get the bail back.

Finally, after about twenty minutes of almost constant signing, they handed me the bond release papers and we were finally able to go.

There were some low angry voices outside of the office, but I didn't care. We were going home, so I pushed the door open and separated the two men there—predictably, Vincent and Kyle.

Dawn was waiting down the hall, in the middle of a gaggle of gay men, and one straight guy. I laughed. She had no idea that she was now officially their mother, and if they ever met Marcus' dad, he was going to be Gaggle Dad.

The highest of honors.

We headed down the hall to the Gaggle, but half way there, I spotted someone on the bench. I thought I was seeing things, but as we got closer, I was sure I wasn't. Holding up a finger to stop Marcus a moment, I walked over to the haggard looking man in jeans and a green polo, with a pair of Chucks... and a baby on his shoulder.

"Felix?"

He jerked his head up and stared at me. "Oh. Hi."

Christ, he looked exhausted. "Are you okay?"

He swallowed. "No."

"What's wrong? What are you doing here?"

"Family court," he said, patting the baby on his shoulder. She let out a little puff of gas, then burped quietly.

"Family court?" I was utterly floored.

"So, yeah," he said, and turned the baby so I could see. "This is Laurie Ann Bich... well. Soon to be Germaine." The sigh he let out was one of a man drained of all physical and emotional strength.

What he said finally hit me.

"She's yours?"

"She is now."

"Felix," I whispered, and put a hand on his shoulder. The little girl was asleep, her blanket curled in her fist and her dark curls just starting to make an appearance. From the way he looked at her, he was in love with the baby, and broken hearted over her as well. "If you need help..."

"Why would you help me?"

"Because we may not be best friends, but that doesn't mean I hate you. It's not my business why you have her, but I don't want you to feel like you can't ask for help."

He swallowed audibly, and I saw tears in his eyes. "Thank you, Chase. That's kind. I'll keep it in mind."

"Germaine?" The name rang down the hall.

He coughed and slipped the baby into the carrier next to him. "If you'll excuse me, I have to sign the papers for my daughter."

Stepping out of the way, I watched as he took everything with him and headed down the corridor. What the hell had happened there?

"Okay?" Marcus asked, slipping in next to me, and putting an arm around my waist.

"Yeah...I just..." I looked at him and blinked a few times. "Did not expect that."

"Life is like that. Unexpected."

I kissed his lips, softly, and gave him a smiled as we turned to head back to the Gaggle at the end of the hall. They were all bouncing on their feet, clearly ready for a free meal.

"I know we have to go feed that lot, but I am so damn ready to go home." Marcus sighed, lacing his fingers in mine.

"Hey, um...speaking of..." I rubbed my neck with my free hand. "Why don't we just make this whole thing official, and um...you know. Kind of..."

"Mingle our dirty laundry?"

"We already do that." I sighed.

"Then there's no reason to keep two hampers, is there?"

I grinned. "Only if we plan on rescuing more wall kittens."

EPILOGUE

MARCUS

October, one year later...

"THANK YOU!" I CALLED OUT TO THE couple walking away from the register. The little rabbit between them took her part seriously, and hopped along, much to the chagrin of her parents.

"Damn she's cute," Chase said. "I also cannot believe those two are parents."

"I can't believe how right you were about this Garcia Pumpkin Patch," I said, opening the register to count out for the day.

The sun was right on the horizon, and the sky was dusky blue and pink and it all faded out over our heads to the first star in the east.

"Venus is rising," Chase teased me.

"First star," I said, ignoring him.

"First *planet*," he corrected.

"Astronomical body." I lifted an eyebrow.

"Why thank you." He laughed.

Shaking my head, I tried not to laugh and lose my count. Chase puttered around, straightening the scales, shutting up the paints and brushes, locking up the carving knives.

With just two more days before Halloween, the pumpkin carving contest was in full swing, too. The entries would be welcomed until six on Halloween, and then the art teacher from the local high school would come by and judge them by nine o'clock Then the pumpkin patch would open again until midnight for a little country fair.

Tomorrow, the patch would be cleared, and all remaining pumpkins moved to a little area in the front for anyone who still wanted to enter the contest or buy a pumpkin. Tomorrow night the fair would be set up—a dunk tank for the high school principal seemed to be the most anticipated.

We'd taken two weeks off this year to help with the end of the pumpkin patch. Last year it had only been one, and it had been apparent they needed us longer than that.

Beth, Tony, and Abuelita had managed most of it, with some help with Rachel, when her mother could watch the baby, or it was a good night to bring her. But October was already chilly and she didn't want the tiny girl out in the cold too much.

Rider was nowhere to be seen, of course. Not while his brother was around.

But tonight, we had close to 200 pumpkins sitting on the hay bales that enclosed the patch, and they were all glowing merrily with fake candles inside. The big lights overhead switched off as I locked up the cash box and handed it off to Beth. She winked and patted my arm.

The only things still glowing as the sun disappeared were the pumpkins and the solar lanterns we had hung around the place for ambiance. It was one of the prettiest sights I'd seen.

Next to my boyfriend, of course.

"One more check for lost hats and gloves?" I asked Chase.

"One more, like we do every night." He motioned me off to the right, and went off the left on his own.

I watched his ass as he walked away. I really did love that ass. I loved the whole man attached to it, so actually the ass was just a bonus.

"Stop staring at my ass," Chase called.

Chuckling I started scanning the ground for lost items. There were always things left behind: scarves, shoes, socks, mittens, even a tiny pair of pants last week, which left us laughing and confused.

I reached into the inside pocket of my jacket and pulled out the little velvet bag. I pinched the circle in my fingers and pulled it out, shoving the bag back in my pocket.

"Oh, man, I found something," I called. "You should see this."

I heard him groan, turn, and head back to the center.

He met me there, and there was mischief in his eyes. Mischief I wanted to be a part of forever.

"Look," I said, and held out the ring.

"Oh, God! That looks expensive! We—"

I was down on one knee when he looked back to find my eyes.

"You bastard," he breathed.

"Marry me, Chase Garcia."

He tried not to let the happy tears fall, but there was no stopping them. "Yes! Yes!"

Under the darkening sky, in the middle of a pumpkin patch, I slipped an engagement ring on the finger of my everything, my guiding star, the man who brought my life out of retrograde forever.

THE STARS HAVE ALIGNED FOR MARCUS AND CHASE...

Want to know when the next star aligns?

Join the S.A. Sommers' Newsletter

AUTHOR'S NOTE

DEAR READERS—

I hope you enjoy Marcus and Chase as much as I did.
The Aligning Stars series is just getting going—there
are a lot of friends who need their happy ending.
Next will be Uriah and Austin, and soon after we'll
find out more about Felix, Noah, Maddox, Kieran,
and Nelson *fucking* Powers.
Please stay tuned! And please follow me on
Facebook, Goodreads, Bookbub and at
sasommer.com. You can also join my newsletter.
Thanks for reading.

S. A. Sommers <3

About
S.A. Sommers

S.A. Sommers has ink in her blood. Sucked into the world of MM Romance by another author, she couldn't resist dipping a toe into the genre and was swept away.

A New Jersey native, she swears like a sailor, has a terrible love for Rutt's Hut, used to sneak into Greenwich Village as a kid and wanted nothing more than to write grand adventures of the human spirit.

Living outside of Philadelphia, she swears (profusely) that you can take the girl out of Jersey, but you can't take the Jersey out of the girl.

Married, Mother of Cats, world traveler, and expert destroyer of dinners, she believes strongly that love is love, and if you have a problem with that, [single finger Jersey salute].

She also writes BDSM, PNR and RH under the name Katherine Rhodes.

(No, really. You haven't lived until you have had a Rutt's Hut ripper.)

By S.A. Sommers

Aligning Stars
Marcus in Retrograde
Uriah's Orbit Coming 1/20/2020
The Battle of Maddox (coming Mar 2020)

Made in the USA
Middletown, DE
25 September 2022